# Ali Sparkes
# UNLEASHED

## THE BURNING BEACH

**OXFORD**
UNIVERSITY PRESS

# For Mia Costello.

## OXFORD
### UNIVERSITY PRESS

Great Clarendon Street, Oxford OX2 6DP
Oxford University Press is a department of the University of Oxford.
It furthers the University's objective of excellence in research, scholarship,
and education by publishing worldwide

Oxford is a registered trade mark of Oxford University Press
in the UK and in certain other countries

First published 2014

British Library Cataloguing in Publication Data

Data available

ISBN: 978-0-19-275610-7

1 3 5 7 9 10 8 6 4 2

Printed in Great Britain

Paper used in the production of this book is a natural,
recyclable product made from wood grown in sustainable forests.
The manufacturing process conforms to the environmental
regulations of the country of origin.

# 1

There was something by the water. Something pale. Moving a little every time the waves came in.

Donal O'Malley paused, his hands full of dark green bladderwrack which mimicked the lumpen outcrops of his elderly knuckles. *It'll be a seal. A dead seal blown ashore in last night's gale,* he told himself. But in his heart, he already knew.

Dropping his harvest onto a shelf of rock, he moved out of the shallow surf as swiftly as his high wader boots would allow and struck out across the firm wet sand. He sent Mary a little prayer—to be wrong. 'Holy Mother of God,' he murmured, barely aware of the words as they slid out past his salt-washed lips. 'Let it be a seal. Please.'

But already he could recognize the angle of a shoulder, a knee, the curve of a hip. It was a woman, then. No—a girl. Slim and young. A teenager. His heart contracted in his chest. He'd seen plenty of death in his time, but it still hit hard when it was a young one. Maybe she'd been out skinny-dipping with friends last night—drunk and silly—and drowned before she knew it. She was as naked as the day she was born, apart from some scraps of dark material on her arms and legs and a few strands of seaweed. Her head lay above the tideline, dark hair blowing in the breeze.

Donal took a steadying lungful of air as he reached the body. Turned away from him, from this angle it looked as if the girl were merely sleeping. He steeled himself to grasp the cold, rigid shoulder, roll the corpse over and gaze upon the nightmare. People who washed up dead on beaches did not look their best. Probably her eyes would be gone.

He gritted his teeth and reached for the shoulder. And as he did so a shriek escaped him. He had been ready for the horrors of a destroyed face—but not for the shock of a living one.

The girl turned her head; her eyes a luminous violet, and stared at him.

'Holy mother of God!' he called out. 'I thought you were dead!'

The girl stared at him some more. Then she said, 'So did I.'

# 2

Donal wrapped his ancient coat around her as she sat up, staring around with those strange, distant eyes. She wasn't shivering even though her skin was as cold as stone.

'What's your name, chick?' he asked.

She mumbled something indistinct. It sounded like Maria.

'Maria, is it? That's a pretty name!' he said. She gazed at him as if she'd never seen a human being before. 'Now then, Maria, I think we've to be getting away indoors now and warming you up. What d'you say to that?'

She blinked but said nothing. He noticed a small red mark on her left cheekbone—a graze or a burn maybe. There were others on her body too, but he did not want to embarrass her by taking a look.

'C'mon then. Let's see if those skinny legs work, shall we? I'd carry you, but I'm a little old for carrying much more than seaweed these days.'

She got to her feet unsteadily and he was able to support her as she walked back up the beach, over the shingle, towards his cave. The sharper stones must have hurt her bare feet but she didn't seem to notice.

He was glad he'd built a little fire before he went out for his first sweep. The weather had been warm all week and not at all rainy until last night. But one good downpour was all it took for the temperature to plunge and his joints to start playing merry havoc with him. So he'd planned to be back before the fire was embers, dump his harvest and have the first cup of tea of the day. Wrapping his stiff fingers around the mug did much to ease the pain.

The cave door was almost rhomboid in shape, as if chiselled out of the slanting stratum of old red sandstone by some giant hand. Inside, the cave roof rose higher and a stream ran merrily down craggy steps beyond the shafts of light edging in from the morning sun. Twisting rivulets of pure spring water fell into a natural basin of rock before gushing on down over the edge and spreading in thin deltas across the sand. The basin was Donal's personal sink—for washing the weed he gathered before dumping it into his cart. The fine waterfall filled his little tin pot for a cup of tea.

Other people occasionally came in; it wasn't truly his alone, but this was a less lovely part of the coast—too much seaweed and rock along this stretch; not enough sand. So mostly the cave was his. This was another thing he was glad of, as he led the girl in and sat her down by the warm circle of pebbles and the pile of smoking peat and driftwood. He added more wood and stuck his tin pot onto the bamboo stick which he'd driven into the sand at an angle, leaving the vessel dangling in the rising heat. The water would boil soon enough. He rinsed his old tin mug and put a fresh teabag into it. Then he moved to the far end of the cave, clambering up onto rocks which looked as if they'd been dropped out of a coal scuttle into the top end of the old cavern. He took it gently— he couldn't be doing with twisting his ankle. Behind the usual rock was his stash of goodies in a large plastic tub. More teabags, sugar, biscuits and some little punnets of UHT milk. Also a spare plastic cup.

The girl was still sitting in silence, her startling eyes following him as he went about his business. When the water boiled he made tea for her, adding three spoonfuls of sugar. Maria—if that's what her name truly was—took the mug passively and wrapped her chilled fingers around it. The steam rose into her face and she blinked her long thick lashes several times.

'Go on! Drink!' Donal urged, and she did, sipping carefully at the sweet brown liquid as if she'd never had it before. 'More,' he said, every time she paused. And every time she went on.

When the tea was halfway down the mug he handed her a digestive. 'Now eat,' he said. She took it and bit an edge off. 'Good—good girl!' he encouraged, as the first hint of colour rose in her cheeks. 'You'll be right as rain, so you will! So . . . how did you come to be washed up here like a mermaid? Can I call someone for you? Sure, your poor mam must be goin' out of her head!'

Maria chewed thoughtfully, narrowing her eyes as if trying to remember, but after a while she just shrugged and went back to eating the biscuit.

'OK, so—let's try something else. D'you know where we are?' He waved around the cavern, picked out in pale blue as the morning light crept further in.

'We're in a cave,' she said. Her voice was soft. English.

'Congratulations!' He grinned as he made tea for himself—adding plenty of sugar. His nerves were still jangling. He needed this tea. 'And where do you think this cave is?'

'I don't know,' she replied.

'What country are we in?'

'I don't know.'

'And what did you say your name was?'

'I can't remember.' She raised her eyes to him and he saw that this last admission troubled her most. 'I should know... shouldn't I?' she said, wiping a damp strand of dark hair off her cheek.

'You said Maria, down on the beach,' he prompted.

'Did I? Maria... ' she tested the word on her tongue. 'That... sounds right.'

'Maria it is then,' said Donal. 'And my name's Donal—pleased to meet you. What about your family—your friends? Can you remember them?'

The girl looked at him blankly for a few seconds and then, like the first few thunder-drops preceding a storm, little puckers of memory rained across her face. Her eyes fluttered and her lips compressed.

He reached out a hand to her arm and she suddenly batted him away.

'NO!'

'What? What is it?' He leaned across to her, trying to lock eyes and somehow see into her troubled mind.

'You mustn't touch!' she hissed, her eyes wide now—warning him.

'I don't mean to hurt you, chick!' he said.

'NO! You don't understand. *I* will hurt *you*!'

'Darlin', I'm sure you wouldn't,' he said, although something in her face made a liar of him. He felt his heart, only just calmed by the tea, begin to rattle in his chest again.

'I won't *mean* to,' she said. 'But that doesn't mean it won't happen.'

'What's happened to you?' he enquired, settling back onto his side of the fire. 'Where's your mam and your dad? Your friends?'

Maria stared at him for several seconds and then murmured. 'Dead.'

'Dead? All of them? Are you sure? Were you in a boat, then? Did you get caught in the storm?'

She nodded slowly. 'A storm,' she murmured. 'There was a storm. But that's not what killed them.'

'What did then, chick?'

'I did.'

# 3

David Chambers took off his rimless spectacles and rubbed the sockets of his eyes. It made the list on his desk go blurry. And frankly, that was a good thing. He did not want to look at the list at all. He wanted it to vanish, along with every other trace of the past twenty-four hours.

Hector, his secretary, came quietly into the room and placed a sandwich and some coffee on his desk. 'You should eat, sir,' he said.

Chambers replaced his glasses and stared at the sandwich—something crusty and no doubt delicious from the Fenton Lodge kitchen—without a flicker of interest. 'Any more?' he asked, waving at the list.

'No, sir,' said Hector, fiddling with his tie. 'Not so far as we can tell. I think it's . . . contained.'

'How, Hector,' snapped Chambers, 'can it *possibly* be contained?'

He saw the young man's throat bob and felt bad. 'I'm sorry—it's not *your* fault. I'm the one to blame. I can't believe I didn't see this coming.'

'Sir,' said Hector, 'if even Lisa Hardman and Paulina Sartre, with their talents, did not see this coming . . . how could you?'

'I may not be psychic,' replied Chambers. 'But two decades in government intelligence ought to stand for something, don't you think? And about Lisa . . . ' he eyed the girl's name on the list, ' . . . any news?'

'Nothing,' murmured Hector.

'Dax Jones?'

'He's gone, sir.'

'Mia Cooper?'

'Gone.'

'Spook Williams?'

'In lockdown. As you ordered.'

'Talking yet?'

'No . . . sir.'

'I have to fly to London,' said Chambers. 'The Prime Minister is holding an emergency council this afternoon. I need *something* to tell him. Something to explain how things have gone so badly wrong on my watch.'

'We're all working on it, sir,' said Hector. 'I've got your travelling bag together.'

Half an hour later, as the helicopter rose high above the Cumbrian country estate which served as the most secure college in the country, Chambers stared down at the smoking patch of ruin near the lodge, thought of that grim list, and wondered, once again, how he had never seen it coming.

# 4

The old man who smelled of seaweed led her along the beach towards some roughly hewn steps in the sloping cliff face. The cliff looked like an ancient domino game tipped over, with wildly slanting strata of grey-red rock. Seabirds flew above their heads with occasional cries as she put one foot steadily in front of the other, following him.

He moved fast for a man of his years—he was surefooted; clearly he knew this path extremely well. But he was suffering. Anyone might have guessed this eventually just from noting the occasional hitch in of breath or a telltale stiffness in his posture, but for Mia, the pain in his joints radiated a feverish heat; she could feel it even several steps behind him. Her instinct to reach out and ease the pain in him was very strong. But a secondary instinct stopped her—and she couldn't quite remember what that was. She must have amnesia. She couldn't remember anything much at all except her name (Mia, not Maria, but Maria would do) and the overriding instinct *not* to touch people. And . . . something about . . . what had she shouted at him in the cave? No. She couldn't remember that either. Not for now.

'Are you all right there?' he enquired, turning and peering back down at her. The early morning sun gave his thinning grey curls a silver halo.

'I'm fine,' she replied. She wasn't. She would never be fine again. Her feet stung from cuts she'd collected as they walked back along the sharp stones. And there were sores (*burns*, whispered an inner voice) on her skin, chafing painfully against the heavy old coat. And she had no clothes of her own—although oddly this caused her little concern. In the overall scheme of things, what did it matter? And the pain was nothing. Any pain she got, she had coming.

They reached the top off the cliff steps and he paused, catching his breath and rubbing one gnarled old hand absently against his hip. 'It's a little further on—not too far,' he assured her. 'Get a bowl of the auld lady's beef broth inside you and you'll be grand in no time.' Mia didn't care about food any more than she'd cared about the tea she'd had in the cave, but her belly seemed to disagree and let out a plaintive, rumbling whine. 'Right, so!' chuckled the old man.

She followed on across the springy green seagrass at the top of the cliff. It wasn't that she *wanted* to follow him—it was just that *not* following him would be harder. He would get anxious and maybe forceful . . . more likely he would go for help. And when help came they would probably lay hands on her and . . . A flash of white light seared across her mind, accompanied by a terrible smell. Burning. Burning hair.

And then it was gone again and still she was following the old man. If he'd looked back he might have seen tears rolling down her cheeks. By the time they reached the old stone-built cottage, though, Mia's face was dry.

'Brigid!' called out Donal as they stepped into a stone porch. The front door was painted dark green. He twisted an iron loop handle on it and pushed it open. 'Brigid!' he called again. 'We have a surprise guest!'

They stepped into a room with stone walls, low wooden beams and a flagstone floor, covered in the centre by a large rug of some faded red and gold pattern. Peat was smoking in a narrow fireplace, filling the air with an earthy perfume. At one end of the room was a wooden table, with four chairs set around it and some flowers in a vase and a stack of books on one end. At the other end, grouped around the fireplace, were two worn brocade armchairs and a sagging leather sofa with many large, dented cushions. There were paintings on the wall—seascapes, mostly—and a small television on a table in one corner.

'Who've you brought, Donal?' called a sing-song voice from a passage which led off behind the dining table area. Seconds later a plump, short woman arrived, dressed in a blue jumper, a flowery skirt, and a striped apron. Her hands were covered in flour and her dark grey hair was knotted back in a bun. 'Well, hello,' she said, her face awash with curiosity.

'This is Maria,' said Donal as cheerfully as if they'd just bumped into each other at a country fair. 'We met on the beach this morning. She's having a small clothing crisis.'

'So I see,' said Brigid, smiling at her. 'And I can't say that auld bundle of rags he still likes to call a coat really suits you.'

Mia looked down at it. It wasn't her best look. Not that she could remember what her best look *was*.

Brigid came across to her and went to put a hand on her shoulder but Mia stepped back quickly. The woman barely missed a beat. She just nodded and smiled. 'I have some old things which should more or less fit you. But maybe you'd like to have a bath first? Get the beach off you?'

Mia nodded. 'Thank you,' she said.

'And are you hungry?'

She nodded again.

'Good—I've a huge pot of beef and potato broth which needs eating. And a fresh batch of soda bread on the way. It'll be just right when you've had your bath.'

Mia caught the woman's questioning glance at Donal as she pointed her along the passage. Donal said nothing but Mia guessed a lot had already passed between them in expression and gesture about the strange girl who'd arrived in their lives that morning.

The passage was whitewashed and several other

rooms led off it. The bathroom was surprisingly elegant, in a simple way. The walls were tiled in white but there was grooved wooden decking on the floor, artfully placed at an angle to the walls—pleasing to the eye. The gleamingly clean toilet and basin were plain enough, but the bath was long and deep, with a rolled top and glistening silver taps. A wooden half barrel stood on the floor at the head end of the bath and a wide shelf, above it, was piled with thick, folded white towels.

'I'll get it sorted for you. The water comes out very hot,' said Brigid, turning both taps on full pelt. The tub began to fill very quickly.

'Will I take Donal's excuse for a coat?' asked Brigid. 'I won't stare, I promise! I've seen all shapes and sizes, trust me,' she added with a chuckle. Mia shrugged off the coat. There was a silence as Brigid took in the marks on her skin.

'Did you get burnt, sweetheart?' she asked, gently.

Mia stared down. The marks were red, turning brown. Some had blisters. They were on her hips and just below her navel, and around her wrists. She could feel, rather than see, those on each of her earlobes.

'No matter,' said Brigid. 'We've just the thing for it!' She left the room at a trot and came back with a bucket. 'It's not as fresh as I'd like—Donal was a bit distracted from this morning's crop, so—but it should do.' And she grabbed something dark green and slippery and slopped it over the edge of the bath. It slithered down into the rising water like a squid. Mia shuddered.

'Sure, it's fine!' Brigid reassured her. 'It's only a bit of seaweed. We put it into the hot water and all its gel comes out and makes the water beautiful. It's the best skin treatment in the world! I should know . . . it's my business!'

She fiddled with the taps some more. 'Normally you'd go in with it piping hot, but we'll cool it down now because of your burns. It'll still do the job. C'mon then—in with you!'

Mia got in, shuddering at first when the strange green tendrils tickled at her feet and ankles.

'I promise there's no wildlife in it!' laughed Brigid. 'People come from far and wide to try my seaweed baths, don't you know? My bathhouse is famous. I've had royalty in it—and nobody's ever found a crab yet!'

Mia sank into the water. The burns on her wrists

stung in the heat and she caught her breath.

'Not too bad?' asked Brigid, busying herself with the towels on the shelf.

'No . . . it's . . . ' Mia paused. What *was* it like? Weird. Not unpleasant. The water was silky smooth and lightly scented with sea minerals. The seaweed drifted with the small tides her body made and seemed to stroke sympathetically at her skin. 'It's . . . OK,' she concluded.

'Good. I'll leave you to it,' said Brigid. 'Don't fall asleep. You can do that after some broth and bread—in a proper bed. I'll make up the guest room for you.'

'Thank you,' said Mia, feeling herself drift along with the seaweed.

'What in God's name has happened to that poor child?' demanded Brigid as soon as she found Donal in the kitchen, leaning on the wooden worktop, raising one shaggy eyebrow at her.

He shrugged. 'I thought she was dead! I found her on the tideline. She was as naked as the day she was born!'

'No clothes lying around anywhere?' asked Brigid. 'No bag—no shoes . . . no clues at all?'

'There were . . . scraps of material on her,' he remembered, screwing up his eyes. 'They looked . . . charred. Like her clothes had been burnt off her. But . . . if so, surely she would be *covered* in burns—I mean, really covered! Not just a few little blisters.'

'Hot metal,' said Brigid. 'Where those marks lay—I'd say it was the metal studs and zip on her jeans . . . bracelet and watch. Earrings. All conducting heat. But no burns from the fire itself?' She shook her head, picked up the tray of soda bread and slid it into the hot oven. 'And what has she told you?'

'Not a lot. Only her name—and that everyone's dead and it's her fault.'

Brigid shut the oven door and turned to him, her face creasing with concern. 'What did she mean by *that*? And did she tell you *who* is dead?'

'No,' sighed Donal. 'I . . . should probably tell you this too . . . the girl's a killer.'

Brigid snorted, 'My backside, old man! That girl couldn't kill a fly!'

'Well . . . *she* thinks she's killed everyone; that's what she told me. D'you think we should call in the Garda?'

'What—that idiot, Finn Malone? Have him clumping in here in his size eleven boots and interrogating her like she's a terrorist? Not on your life!'

'I didn't mean *him*,' said Donal, running some warm water into the white ceramic sink so he could soothe his aching fingers in it. 'I was thinking of the proper Garda, up in Tralee, maybe. A female, perhaps. A specialist in these things. The girl's obviously traumatized. And her family must be out of their minds with worry—we ought to report this.'

Brigid considered. 'Let's see what we can do for her first,' she said. 'I don't want to rush her out of here. I think . . . I think she needs to be here for a while.'

Donal raised an eyebrow. Brigid was a sensible, down to earth woman, but she did have her 'intuitions'. Donal had to admit, though, that she was usually right.

'Don't give me that look, old man!' she said, but she knew he agreed with her anyway. It was there in the set of his shoulders. 'Let's see how she shapes up after some food and rest and then we can decide. Now—I've bread to see to—and I think there's some barrels waiting to be stocked with seaweed, or are we declaring a national holiday in honour of finding naked forgetful girls on beaches?'

# 5

'*What* did you call her?' asked the Prime Minister, sitting forward fast enough to make his high-backed leather chair creak.

Chambers, sitting opposite, docked his teacup with its saucer on the closest side of the PM's vast walnut desk and repeated the word. 'I just wish I had known,' he went on. '*Now* it all seems abundantly obvious. The signs were there. I should have worked out what she was *years* ago.'

'Maybe so,' said the PM. 'But I'm not interested in your personal agonizing, Chambers. What I want is your professional opinion. Is she still alive? And if so—is she a threat?'

'I can't give you satisfactory answers, Prime Minister,' sighed Chambers. 'She's a Child Of Limitless Ability ... which means we don't know what her limits *are*. She has vanished, like the other COLAs did earlier this summer; you remember—Spook Williams first and then Jacob and Alex Teller. But I don't know if she was taken by the same person, in the same way. Neither can I confirm that she's dead, although . . . ' he rubbed the bridge of his nose and looked, for a second, desperately sad, ' . . . it might be better if she was.'

'Can't your mediums and dowsers tell you that?' snapped the PM. 'Surely if she'd popped up in the afterlife word would have got back by now. What about your COLA, Lisa Hardman, eh? The best dowser and psychic medium we have if I remember correctly? What is *she* telling you?'

Chambers wasn't surprised the PM remembered Lisa. She had helped to save his life after all, and besides, people who met Lisa rarely forgot her. 'Lisa Hardman is no longer able to help us,' he said.

The PM's grey eyes widened before he sat back, looking slightly winded. 'She's . . . ' he indicated the list of names on his desk, ' . . . on this?'

Chambers nodded.

'Mia's *best friend?*'

He nodded again. 'And the other dowsers and mediums have been unable to offer us anything useful so far,' said Chambers. 'But they're still very young, not so powerful—and in shock.'

'This is a mess,' muttered the PM. 'What are you doing about it?'

'We have every available operative searching for Mia, but when what we've seen recently simply . . . violates the laws of physics . . . it's no easy task.'

'So . . . you think the rogue COLA—the teleporting boy . . . what's his name?'

'Olu Jackson, sir.'

'This Olu Jackson—you think *he's* involved again? Snatching COLAs off into some other dimension on the orders of your old friend Marcus Croft?'

'As far as we know,' said Chambers. 'Olu Jackson is dead. He fell off a cliff into the sea—apparently unable to teleport and save himself. And two weeks later a body fitting his description washed ashore five miles up the coast. But . . .'

'But?' prompted the PM.

'We have no DNA or dental records for Olu Jackson—nothing which could help us to properly ID the body. And Marcus Croft did vanish around the time Olu fell. It's possible the boy found a way to teleport at the last second and take Croft with him. And for the record, sir, Croft is no friend of mine.'

'Noted,' said the Prime Minister, with the raise of one eyebrow. 'But he knows you well, regardless. Along with many of your old colleagues in MI5. And he seems set upon acquiring more COLAs.'

'Oh yes,' breathed Chambers, remembering his meeting with the man a few weeks back and shuddering. 'And I wouldn't put it past him to kill a teenager who fitted Olu's description, just so he could dump the body in the sea for us to find.'

The PM grimaced. 'So—it *could* be Croft using Olu Jackson still . . . or it could be something else . . . Maybe there are more teleporters out there.'

Chambers nodded. This terrible thought had occurred to him too.

'Could Mia Cooper have left the Fenton Lodge estate any other way?' asked the PM.

Chambers frowned. 'In theory—no. But that's just the point, sir—all we have, when it comes to Children Of Limitless Ability, *is* theory . . . based on what we have learned about them so far. Clearly some can develop unexpected abilities. Who knew that Mia Cooper, the gentlest creature I ever met—a *healer*—could do *this?*'

He and the PM both allowed their eyes to roam the large colour prints spread across his desk. They showed a charred wasteland; the steps to Fenton Lodge blackened and decorated with weird twists of melted wrought iron balustrade, the hedges beneath them turned to sticks of charcoal in a thick drift of ash; sooty windows framing buckled and blown glass.

'The teleporter—*if* a teleporter *was* involved—has a weakness,' said Chambers, pulling his eyes away from the prints. 'He cannot port while in contact with this.' He pulled a small lump of gleaming grey-black mineral from his jacket pocket. 'Magnetite. It protects other people from being ported too. All COLAs have been wearing magnetite bracelets since late last month. And we had just finished a programme of inserting a lozenge of magnetite into their palms—*here.*' He indicated the plump area beneath his left thumb where his own magnetite lay.

'Just *finished?* Why did it take so long?' asked the PM. 'Surely this was something which you should have done *immediately?*'

'With respect, sir,' said Chambers, 'it's not quite that simple. We needed the fathers to sign consent. Remember the trouble we had with the tracker chips?'

The PM compressed his lips, nodding. He remembered it well. An ill-thought-out security exercise which had nearly killed eleven COLAs less than two years ago.

'Since then, we find it's best to keep the families in the loop as far as possible,' explained Chambers. 'It took a while to get agreement.'

'And Mia Cooper's father? Did he agree?' asked the PM.

'Ah,' said Chambers. 'He didn't get the chance.'

'Are you telling me *he's* on this list too?' demanded the PM, picking up the paper and shaking it.

'Edward Cooper is dead,' said Chambers. He uncovered another photograph which showed a human shape in a blackened bed. The PM instinctively covered his mouth with one hand.

'And I think,' said Chambers, 'this is where it all started.'

# 6

The beef and vegetable broth was good. Mia finished the entire bowl, with two heavy slices of warm soda bread, spread thickly with cool butter.

'Well, you look a *lot* better!' said Brigid. 'How are your burns?' She reached across the scrubbed pine kitchen table to turn Mia's wrist but Mia swiftly withdrew her hand.

'Y'know, I've no intention of hurting you,' said Brigid. 'Are you scared of me, chick? Am I that ugly?'

A ghost of a smile touched the girl's lips as she shook her head.

'Then is it the poor fashion sense?' went on Brigid, smiling at the clothes her guest now wore—a shapeless fleecy green top and some beige trousers which stopped a little short of her ankles.

'You're very kind,' said Mia. 'And I don't want to seem ungrateful. But you have to let me go now. I'm not good for you. I hurt people.'

'Oh—and how do you do that?' asked Brigid.

'I . . . ' Mia's eyes clouded. 'I don't remember how. I just know it's true.'

'But why would you *want* to hurt me?' asked Brigid, frowning slightly as she tried to understand.

'I don't want to!' said Mia. 'It just . . . happens.'

'So . . . where will you go?' Brigid asked, scooping up the last of her broth with a round spoon. A covered pot of it sat on the kitchen stove, awaiting the return of Donal, who had gone back to the beach to collect his abandoned seaweed.

Mia said nothing. Where *would* she go? What was her plan? She couldn't think. She only knew she had to be away from people. As soon as possible.

'Look, why don't you sleep on it?' suggested Brigid. 'Maybe a plan will come along in your dreams.'

'Yes,' said Mia, thinking of the bedroom she'd been shown into after the seaweed bath, with its crisp cotton sheets on a firm, high bed, 'please. That would be very kind . . . before I go.'

'That's settled then,' said Brigid, getting up and

gathering the empty bowls and plates. 'And don't be worrying yourself about anyone else dropping in. We keep ourselves to ourselves around here. You'll be quite safe.'

'I know,' said Mia. And for the first time she smiled properly at Brigid.

Brigid got to her feet to put the butter in the fridge. She was suddenly filled with warmth. The girl's eyes were quite something. Violet blue . . . like Elizabeth Taylor's in *National Velvet*. The tension headache which had been nagging behind Brigid's eyes melted away.

*If I were more religious,* thought Brigid, *I might fancy that was an angel sitting there at my table.*

Donal arrived back. 'I've filled the barrels—you'll be grand for this afternoon,' he said. 'I hope you've not gone and had all the broth out from under me!'

'Of course not,' said Brigid, turning back to the stove. 'Give yourself a wash, so. Remember we've company.'

'I'm not likely to forget it,' chuckled Donal, moving to the sink, grabbing a yellow sliver of coal tar soap and holding his hands under the hot tap. Mia noticed the way his face puckered a little as the water played across his fingers. She could see that they were swollen at the knuckles—worse than first thing that morning. She knew that arthritis could flare up fast. Her own hands tingled with warmth, ready to assist. The urge to get up and go to him was building with every second that passed. She clenched her fists and stared down at the table. No. NO.

And yet the healing flowed out of her regardless. She didn't need to lay hands on him or even focus her energy in his direction. It was leaking out of her, streaming in golden plumes of light from her hands and her mouth and her solar plexus. *Stop it!* she told herself and the stream of energy dissipated.

'Aaah, that's better,' sighed Donal, at the sink. 'Nothing like hot water after a cold rummage through the ocean's armpits!'

He sat at the table opposite her and flexed his fingers. 'Y'know, it's not so bad, today,' he murmured. 'Not so bad at all.'

'Will you take the crop on up to the bathhouse after?' asked Brigid, filling the washing-up bowl.

'We've seven bookings—and there may be a few walk-ins if the sun stays out.'

Donal looked at his watch. 'Time enough, woman! Let me get some broth down me!'

'You have . . . a bathhouse?' Mia was curious, in spite of her instinct to stay remote from these temporary friends.

'We have the most famous seaweed baths in Ireland!' announced Brigid. 'Well . . . second-most famous, maybe—the baths at Ballybunion probably get a little more attention. But we do nicely enough. I've had Hollywood stars take my seaweed baths, don't you know?'

'Oh,' said Mia. She looked at her wrists. The burns were definitely soothed and her skin felt smooth and silky. 'So . . . people come here . . . for seaweed baths?'

'Not here,' said Brigid, quickly. 'Up at the bathhouse—about a quarter of a mile north of here, on the sandy part of the beach, where all the tourists stop. We run it with a little shop and tea room too. We've a couple of lovely ladies who work there, along with Donal and me.'

As she folded herself into the cool, fresh-smelling cotton sheets of the guest room bed twenty minutes later, Mia was struck again by the old couple's restraint. They must be agog to know who she was and how she had washed up on their beach that morning like a troublesome bit of driftwood. Helping her as they were, they had some right to know, she guessed.

She would tell them if she could—but every time she tried to focus, her mind seemed to crackle and glitch and go fuzzy, like an old television with no aerial. And with the crackling, glitching fuzz came a swell of panic and misery. Something terrible had happened. People had died. She didn't know what and she didn't know who . . . she just knew it was her fault.

The food and the warmth of the bed gradually eased her into sleep. Slowly, slowly, her muscles relaxed and her eyelids drooped and her fingers uncurled on the pillow beside her cheek. Sleep came. And with it came dreams.

*'You're not like them,' said the amber-eyed boy. 'They don't understand you like I do.'*

*'They do!' she protested. 'They know me very well. And they still like me—ha ha!'*

*The boy stared down at her and ran one finger along her cheek. 'You're not like them,' he said again. 'Or else why would you be here . . . with me? Would they ever talk to me like this? Would they ever look at me . . . like you do?'*

*She gulped and brushed his hand away, but in doing so caught his fingers and held on as their hands dropped.*

*'You see the world differently,' he continued. 'And you are not what they think you are.'*

*She glanced up at him sharply.*

*'They think you're a walking feel-good kit,' said the boy. 'The world's best healer. What they don't understand is what it takes. What it costs you. Yes— they see that you feel the pain you take from other people and that it wrings you out for a while . . . but it's not that which messes you up, is it? It's what you're hiding from them . . . what's on the flipside of sweet, gentle Mia.'*

*She stepped away, watching the evening sun glint on his dark red hair and put flames in his eyes. But he moved across and pulled her close to him, pressing her cheek to his chest so she could feel the steady thud of his heart through his silky black sweater.*

*'I know what's on the flipside and I still accept you— kill or cure,' he whispered into her hair. 'I know you're Cure. And I know you're Kill.'*

\*

In the kitchen Donal and Brigid talked quietly over a cup of tea. They heard Maria, in her sleep, call out, 'No . . . no I don't want . . . ' and then rejoin her dream world in silence.

'So what next?' asked Donal, after a pause. 'You're never going to let her wander off, are you?'

'Of course not,' said Brigid. 'Don't worry—she'll stay.'

'I'm not to worry, leaving you alone in the house with a mass murderer?' Donal was only half joking.

'She's a good girl,' said Brigid. 'Can't you *feel* it?'

Donal stared at his wife for a few seconds, one eyebrow raised, but he didn't lapse into the usual mickey-taking—because he *could* feel it. From the moment he had touched the girl and brought her to his cave, he had felt it. Something extraordinary. It was like drawing close to a bonfire on a bitter December night.

'Give me time and I'll get her to talk,' said Brigid.

'But what if she has, y'know, amnesia? All memory knocked out of her by a blow to a head? She should see a doctor.'

Brigid nodded. 'Yes, she should. Maybe tomorrow. I've been thinking about that. We could ask for a house call . . . say you're not so grand and need a look over. Dr Keyes would come for that, wouldn't he? And then, once he was here, we could get him to look at her.'

'She won't like it,' said Donal. 'She might run.'

'Tomorrow . . . or the next day,' said Brigid. 'She just needs time—whatever's happened to her. Time.'

They nodded at each other and silence, apart from the occasional pop and hiss of the kitchen wood burner, reigned for a few seconds. Then their guest called out from her dreams again—only this was surely a nightmare because the horror and misery in Maria's scream made the hairs stand up on Donal's arms.

'Nooooo! Oh nooo! I'm sorry—I'm so sorry.'

They opened the door and stood quietly, shoulder to shoulder, staring down at her in the dim light filtering through the drawn curtains. She was deeply asleep and no good would be done by waking her. The girl's pale brow was furrowed and her dark hair streaked across her face, damp with tears.

'Come for me, Dax,' she murmured. 'Shift. And rip out my throat if you still can.'

After that, she said no more.

# 7

'Give me the bag, Señor, and you will live.'

Tyrone Lewis froze, the cold edge of a blade across his throat. The man behind was shorter than him, but muscular and reeking of old sherry and fried onions. He felt certain it was the guy in the red T-shirt who had stared at him in the taverna. He cursed his urge for that cool beer. He should have headed straight home.

'Don't do anything stupid,' hissed the man. 'Or I'll slit your throat.'

Tyrone sighed. 'Define stupid,' he said, in Spanish, clamping the battered leather satchel against his chest. It contained a month's wages in cash. He really could not let it go. 'Attempting a handstand? Farting the national anthem with a chicken on my head? Making that bicycle do a little dance?'

'Uh?' His mugger was thrown. He expected this skinny lad, barely out of his teens, to be quaking with fear and scrabbling to hand over his bag. He didn't expect backchat.

He also didn't expect a bicycle to do a little dance.

The battered old red gents' racer was now up on its back wheel, shimmying back and forth between the tall metal waste bins. Rearing up into a riderless wheelie, the machine began to spin in the dusty alleyway.

'Uh?' repeated the mugger and the second his shocked hand drifted away from his victim's throat, Tyrone flexed his mind again, twisting the blade out of the mugger's fingers and sending it high into the air.

The man squawked, his eyes wild above the red cotton scarf which he'd knotted across his nose and mouth. The knife rose high above his head and the blade slowly bent over on itself until the weapon resembled a potato peeler. Staring, aghast, he didn't even notice Tyrone move across the narrow alley.

Tyrone let the knife drop to the floor and this seemed to release the man from his enchantment. He whirled around and made a grab for the bag, cursing with venom. 'I don't think so,' said Tyrone, and flipped the bike 360 degrees through the air onto the mugger's head.

The man collapsed, yelling, beneath the spinning wheels, clicking gears and shuddering mudguards, one pedal striking him hard enough across the brow to break the skin. Tyrone didn't stop to watch. He legged it out of the alleyway and as soon as he'd turned the corner, dropped into a swift walk, whistling softly to himself. Plenty of people saw him in the evening shade; but virtually nobody actually *saw* him. They were occupied with late shopping or checking the menus outside the tavernas or flirting with the girls who stood around the square in short skirts. Tyrone was just some guy, keeping his head down.

His actions may have been unwise . . . but if you couldn't use telekinesis to defend yourself from a knife-wielding robber, what *was* it for? The mugger had been drunk—nobody would believe his story, if he told it. And it was unlikely he would. No Spaniard would admit he'd been bested by some skinny English kid. Tyrone had picked up the tan and the language but he knew he still looked and sounded English. There was no point in denying it to the people he did casual labour for. He told them he was a student on a gap year, working to pay his way while he improved his Spanish. Nobody ever queried this.

On the outskirts of the small town he found his own bike—a decent all-terrain job—carefully hidden in the dusty scrub beside the road that led out into the mountains. Tyrone pulled the bike out, detached the helmet and goggles; put them on. The helmet was hell on his hair but he'd given up caring long ago. A couple of tumbles in the mountains taught you the value of some head gear—and the goggles protected his eyes from the dust his regular skids kicked up. The hat and goggles combo also meant that people didn't remember his face if they saw him pass.

He mounted and soon picked up speed, glad to be leaving the lights and the lowlife of Palera well behind him. Few cars passed him and they were all going into town. Soon he was off the main road and onto one of the many hard-packed earth tracks which led deeper into the mountains. He wrangled his metal steed confidently up sandy tracks, over rocky precipices and down through cactus-choked gullies which hadn't seen a drop of water in two months. The heat of the day radiated from the baked earth and sand lizards still scurried across his path, but the air was rapidly cooling as night stole across the eastern sky. Back home he would be glad of the fire. His housemate would surely have got it going and with any luck was preparing fajitas for the skillet right now.

Tyrone turned the corner of a familiar limestone outcrop and braked so hard his rear wheel bucked behind him. The bike flipped like a temperamental mare. Tyrone sprawled in the gritty soil, one elbow collecting spines from a squat khaki cactus. Standing on a shelf of rock beside the track was a fox.

It wasn't because this fox was staring at him, rather than darting away into the gloom, that Tyrone tingled from head to foot. It wasn't even the almost human way that it tilted its head and regarded him with interest.

No. It was something else entirely. Something unmissable.

Both of them were alone at twilight on a remote mountain track in Southern Spain.

And both of them were from England.

Tyrone picked himself up, wiping grit from his

stinging palms, and stared at the creature before him. It wasn't the sandy-to-charcoal colour of a Spanish fox. It was red. A fox with a thick auburn pelt and a lustrous white bib of fur from its throat to its chest. It continued to sit and regard him, its bushy tail curled around its feet, as if waiting for him to speak.

Tyrone took three steps forward, pulling off his goggles, thinking it *might* run, yet knowing that it wouldn't. Goosebumps rose on him. The world slowed down. A grin spread across his face, revealing even white teeth.

'Hey, Dax,' he said. 'Good to see you.'

# 8

The man at the wood burning stove laced thin strips of beef and chunks of red onion and pepper along wooden skewers. He placed the latest kebab on a metal tray with the others, shoved a stray lock of shaggy dark hair out of his eyes, and glanced at his watch. Ty should be back any time now. Should he get the kebabs on?

Despite this domestic scene, evidence of his former life was everywhere. The cave house was neat, clean, and well ordered. It had heating, hot and cold running water, and an amazing array of weaponry. Two Glocks in cubby holes behind the wine rack and boot trunk, a shotgun above the saucepans which hung from the ceiling, smoke grenades at the back of the under-sink cupboard; even throwing knives magnetized to the insides of the metal uplighters on the walls. He and Tyrone had trained rigorously over the past two years—and memorized the layout of the caves and what could be found where. In the event of attack, the defences at their disposal were considerable—and always to hand. If you knew what you were looking for it was a giant game of Where's Weapon Wally.

But there had been no attack and sometimes it seemed like there would never be. Maybe he and Ty would just potter on here undisturbed for decades, the odd couple. Well, until Ty fell in love with a Spanish girl, he guessed, and began to long for a normal life. Then he would have to rethink everything.

The skillet was hot enough now. His drop of olive oil jumped across the pan with a hiss. Time to put the kebabs on. There were four each. Was that enough?

As if to answer, Tyrone arrived back. There was the clunk and drag of his bike being pulled inside. 'How many kebabs you got on?' he called.

'Eight,' called back the cook.

'Better add a few more,' called Ty, shoving open the screen door, bringing dust and the scent of the mountains in with him.

And a fox. He brought in . . . a fox.

'We have a guest,' said Ty, smiling.

Owen Hind stood motionless beside the sizzling stove. He felt his world slow down and blood rush noisily through his ears. What rose through his chest he didn't at first recognize, but as soon as the fox shifted, into a wiry, dark-haired, dark-eyed teenage boy, he realized what it was.

Joy.

'God alive,' was all he said, in a voice thick with emotion. 'You found us.'

The boy gave him a tired, lopsided grin. He seemed to be struggling for words. Owen took three strides across the room and swept him into a hug.

'Dax Jones. It is so good to see you!'

Dax hugged him back hard and then stepped away, his face mirroring his former teacher's delight and then becoming more serious. 'You said to come . . . when I needed you.'

'And you need me?'

'Owen,' said Dax. 'We *all* need you.'

Tyrone moved quickly across to the stove and saved them from a fajita fire, as man and boy continued to gawk at each other. 'For what it's worth,' he said. 'I think these fajitas will be enough for three.' He winkled some floury tortillas out of a paper bag on the thick stone worktop and put them onto a tin plate, to warm up on the back of the stove. 'Dax hasn't eaten anything but one unlucky pigeon since yesterday, so let's sort that out first, eh?'

Owen grinned, shaking his head. 'Some things never change! Still ravenous after a shift?'

'Always,' said Dax, grinning back.

Owen could see that much was weighing on the boy, but in spite of it, he was elated to be back in old company. The bond between them had not loosened over the past two years, since his 'death'. Owen felt a quickening inside him. Just five minutes ago he had been musing on the aimless state of his life, hidden away in the Spanish mountains, but now it seemed he was back in play.

'How did you find us?' he asked. 'The map?'

Dax grinned and pulled a thin, crackling map from his pocket. Owen had given this to him, rolled up and hidden in the barrel of a pencil, in case he ever needed to find him. Being officially 'dead', his whereabouts could never be advertised.

Tyrone brought the sizzling kebabs, the tortillas,

and some sour cream and guacamole to the old wooden table. In minutes they were all eating enthusiastically, chasing the fajitas down with chilled apple juice. The colour returned to Dax's face. Neither Tyrone nor Owen pushed Dax on what had prompted him to travel hundreds of miles to find them. They knew to wait.

Eventually, clunking his empty glass tumbler back down on the table, Dax took a breath and let it out again slowly. Then he raised his eyes to Owen's and said: 'Mia's gone.'

'Where?' asked Owen, lines creasing his brow.

'We don't know. But it's worse than that.'

'Can't Lisa find her?' interjected Owen. 'They're best friends! Surely Lisa can dowse her . . . I . . . I'm not getting the picture, am I, Dax?' he tailed off, realizing that his questions were fatuous. Why would Dax be here if Lisa could find Mia?

'Lisa can't dowse anyone,' said Dax, and his eyes flickered and dropped to the table in front of them.

Owen felt a coldness slip across his full belly. 'Dax . . . tell me what happened.'

Dax's face rippled with pain. 'We got Mia wrong, Owen. We didn't understand.'

'How—how did we get her wrong?' Owen saw

the girl in his mind—warmth, kindness, and grace personified—and couldn't grasp what Dax was telling him.

'She's not just a healer, Owen,' muttered Dax. 'That's just one side of her. I . . . I've known it for a long time but I thought it would be OK. Maybe if I'd done something sooner . . . '

Owen rested his chin on his knuckles. 'What is she, Dax? What *else* is she?'

Dax met his gaze; guilt, misery, and horror chasing across his face. 'She's a killer.'

# 9

Mia woke around seven the next morning. Light was filtering through a crack in the green curtains to the left of her bed. With it came the scent and the sound of the sea. She remembered where she was. She must have slept right around the clock! She got up and pulled an oversized flannel robe around her before shuffling to the bathroom to ease her bladder and have a wash. In the mirror above the gleaming white sink she regarded her face with mild curiosity. It was not as pale as yesterday, when she'd glanced into the glass before getting into the seaweed bath. Her violet eyes were large and luminous in the white light and her mouth was now pink, rather than ivory. She traced long, lean fingers across the pale marks on her throat. They were *much* paler. Had she done that herself? Finally learned how to self-heal? Or was it just magic seaweed? She smiled at the thought.

Her hair was awful, though. She found a hairbrush in a wall cabinet, amid medicines and pots of skin cream. She dragged it through the dark brown mass, tugging out knots and clumps until it looked . . . well . . . OK. She noticed a new toothbrush, still in its packet, inside the cabinet. She guessed it would be all right to use it, so she unwrapped it and put it to work with some old-fashioned-looking toothpaste which tasted of eucalyptus. Not like the minty stuff at the lodge.

'What's *the lodge*?' she asked herself, aloud. In the mirror her brow creased as if it was remembering. It wasn't. Not yet.

When she got back to the bedroom she found Brigid waiting with a carrier bag. 'How are you?' asked the woman. 'We didn't want to wake you for food last night—you seemed to need the sleep more.'

'I—I'm better. Thank you,' said Mia.

'I went into town,' said Brigid. 'Picked up some nicer clothes for you. Can't have you wandering around in my cast-offs, looking like a scarecrow!' She upended the bag on the bed and a pair of blue jeans, some khaki cargo pants, and a couple of sweatshirts slid out; one green, one lilac. 'I thought this would work well with your lovely eyes,' said Brigid, smiling as she plucked at the lilac top.

'You're very kind,' mumbled Mia. 'I don't deserve it.'

'Ah, don't go on so,' urged Brigid. 'It's years since I had an excuse to go girly clothes shopping. I loved it! Even got you some frillies, look!' She pointed to a three-pack of white cotton and lace knickers and a matching bra. 'No idea of your size, of course—had to guess. Guessed the boots too . . .' She indicated a cardboard box on the carpet, with a new three-pack of black ankle socks resting on it. 'A six, are you?'

'You know . . . I'm going soon . . . today,' said Mia, feeling a flush steal across her face. 'There's no need.'

'Look—if you're going to wander away with a little spotted hanky on a stick filled with bread and ham, you'll not want to be doing it in granny's clothes that don't fit,' insisted Brigid. 'If it ever gets out that you stopped over at the O'Malley's and we let you leave looking like that, sure, we'd never live it down!' She flapped the tops in the air. 'So go on, now—humour an old lady. Try them on!' And she left the room with her request hanging in the air.

Mia did. It felt comforting to wear normal clothes again. Brigid had guessed well—everything was a good fit; even the bra. She put on the lilac top because she knew that was the one Brigid most wanted to see her in. In the mirror over an old dark wood dressing table her eyes looked like amethyst with the colour of the top reflecting in them. The grey suede walking boots, as she eased her freshly socked feet into them, were also correctly guessed.

'I'd like to do something . . . to pay for these,' she said, as she emerged into the kitchen. Donal, she sensed, was out. There were no vibes of arthritic pain in the house.

Brigid turned, a kettle in her hand, and smiled warmly. Very warmly.

*The Effect,* thought Mia with a small knot in her insides. *Here we go. She'll tell me I don't need to do anything—that it's her pleasure. And she won't even know why.*

But she misjudged Brigid. 'Well, you know . . . ' said the woman, ' . . . they did set me back a bit. A shift or two at the bathhouse should cover it.'

'Oh,' said Mia, genuinely surprised. This was new.

'Of course, it'll mean you'll have to stay a couple of days longer before you . . . you know . . . wander off with your hanky and stick.'

'Well—if you're sure I won't inconvenience you . . . ' murmured Mia, sinking down onto a seat at the small table. Her single plan—to get away from people—was getting a bit lost. She should just go. Here and now. But the wind buffeted the kitchen window and the sea was steely grey, giving her no illusions about how cold it would be out there right now. And that smelt very much like porridge on the stove. She could at least get some hot food inside her before she went.

'Maria,' said Brigid, sitting down opposite her. 'Let me be frank with you. I don't *want* you to go. Not before we've found your family . . . or your guardians . . . or anyone at all that might be missing you. Is there anyone? Can you remember now?'

Mia shook her head. 'I can't remember much at all but I know that there is . . . *nobody.*'

'Was it a shipwreck? Were you out on a yacht or something?' asked Brigid.

Mia shrugged. 'I don't think so. I don't think I . . . go on yachts.'

'Donal thinks there was a fire,' said Brigid. 'He

found charred bits of material around you on the beach—and there are these.' She pointed to the fading marks. '*Well*—the seaweed worked wonders!' she marvelled, and Mia allowed her to touch the pale scar on her wrist. 'Do you remember a fire?'

An image of white heat seared across her memory, along with the crackle of wood and the smell of burning hair. Inside she flinched and part of her mind whimpered, *I'm sorry!* but on the outside she merely blinked a few times. 'I don't know . . . there may have been. Must have been, I suppose.'

'So . . . ' said Brigid. 'We have your name—Maria—yes?' Mia smiled and did not correct her. 'And we know you're not from around these parts . . . You've an English accent . . . southern, I'd say. Maybe from somewhere around London?'

'Maybe,' Mia agreed.

'You seem to be fit and well—apart from the burns and the memory loss. And somebody *must* be looking for you,' concluded Brigid. 'The question is . . . do you want to be found?'

'No,' said Mia. 'Definitely not.'

'So you say and you seem mighty certain,' said Brigid. 'But you've no idea why . . . ?'

'None at all,' said Mia. 'It's just . . . instinct.'

Brigid looked at her for some seconds. 'Well—I suppose you'll tell me when you're ready.'

Mia nodded. 'If I remember, before I—'

'Go—yes, before you go,' smiled Brigid. 'Well—how do you feel about coming up to the bathhouse with me? You can make a start on working off the clothes and boots and meet my lovely ladies. Now, don't look so worried, we'll tell them you're a friend of my niece's come over from London to stay and study Irish culture!' laughed Brigid. 'I'll tell them to lay off the questions as they're a nosey bunch, to be sure. Just say you're a student, doing . . . I don't know . . . Celtic History. That should do it!'

'OK,' Mia agreed. 'And what work will I do?'

'We'll teach you to run the till, take the money for the baths, serve the tea and cakes, clean up, prepare the baths . . . all of it. But not all at once—no need to look so scared!'

They reached the bathhouse in Brigid's elderly, muddy Land Rover, bumping along a narrow cliff track from the cottage until they joined a tourist road and headed north on tarmac. Wiry grass undulated along the clifftop and the grey sea glinted and grew bluer as the sun broke through the clouds. On Brigid's side the land rose to breathtaking heights, vibrantly green, patterned with low stone walls, hardy looking sheep, and occasional stone huts which looked as if they had sprung from the soil like grey mushrooms.

'We call those "beehives" on account of their shape,' Brigid informed as they drove past one. 'They're scattered around the place—some as old as the hills. Some right up in the mountains, too—they've saved a few day-trippers from exposure, so I hear.'

They turned at a signpost for **BRANNIGAN BEACH**. Further down its pole was a notice reading: *O'MALLEY'S SEAWEED BATHHOUSE, TEA, COFFEE & CAKES.* And beneath that: BERNIE'S BEACHWARE & GIFTS and: **PUBLIC CONVENIENCE**.

They bumped down the steep, winding road and pulled onto a rutted track which led behind a single storey whitewashed building with a steeply pitched tiled roof. 'This is us,' said Brigid, getting out. Mia followed, glad of her thick-soled walking boots as she jumped down onto the stony track. She also had on a borrowed fleecy zip-up jacket which kept the cool sea breeze at bay as she followed Brigid to the building. A wooden painted sign above the door proclaimed: *O'MALLEY'S SEAWEED BATHHOUSE & TEA ROOM (APPOINTMENTS NOT ALWAYS NECESSARY, COME INSIDE AND ASK)*.

Below the bathhouse was a concrete hardstanding which led on to the gift shop and, further along, to a public toilet. Picnic tables were set out along the hardstanding and maybe forty or fifty people were roaming this and the wide beach beyond. Mia spotted more of those strange 'collapsed domino' cliffs and dark yawning caves within them. Seabirds cried out overhead and a sea-scented gust of wind swept her hair back off her face.

'Not bad for a place of work, is it?' said Brigid, lightly touching Mia's shoulder to guide her inside. Mia realized she was forgetting to keep her distance. But no harm seemed to have come to the older woman so far. Maybe she didn't need to worry . . .

Inside the building was a corridor off to the right, with four wooden doors. *These must be the bathing cubicles*, Mia worked out, noting the wooden slat mats at the front of each of them and the sound of running water behind the doors.

'I'll show you the baths in a while, but first come in and meet Niamh and Mary,' said Brigid, turning left into a small, stone-floored tea room. There were six tables, with cheerful red-checked vinyl tablecloths. The chairs around most of these were occupied by customers, consuming hot or cold drinks and cakes, scones or sandwiches. Two women were stationed behind the high glass counter above the cake and sandwich display. One was working at a marble slab, cutting up fruit cake with a long, sharp knife, and the other was at the till.

'This is Niamh,' said Brigid, indicating the slim red-haired woman on cake-cutting duty who looked around thirty, 'and Mary.' A mousy-haired woman of stouter build who was probably ten years older, Mia guessed. Both women gave her friendly and curious smiles, glancing quickly at Brigid, eyebrows raised. 'Hello,' they chorused.

'And this is Maria—a friend of Kathy's!' said Brigid. 'Come all the way from London to spend a while with Donal and me—for her studies, would you believe!'

'What's she studying?' asked Mary. 'Seaweed millionaires, is it?' She guffawed along with Brigid and Niamh joined in readily.

'Our regular joke,' explained Brigid. 'No—she's doing something Celtic,' went on Brigid. 'But don't you be clubbing her poor pretty head in with questions—she just wants to observe the proper west coast way of life. And she's willing to work for it too—so we'll be training her up.'

'Oh-ho!' grinned Niamh, returning to her cake cutting. 'That's grand, Maria. We'll be putting our feet up and letting you take the strain, then!' And then the knife slipped.

Niamh let out a gasp followed by a muffled curse, grabbing her hand up to her chest, blood dripping from it.

'Oh no—that's deep!' said Mary, at her side in an instant. 'What were you thinking of, you great donkey?!'

Niamh winced as she uncovered the wound. Mia could see it *was* deep—a stitches job, no question. And before she was even aware of what she was doing she had slipped around the till and reached for Niamh, pulling the cut hand into her own and pulsing in a wave of healing.

Nobody stopped her. The three women just stared as she went to work and she realized that a great cloud of Mia Effect had rolled out of her and engulfed them all. They looked hazy and confused . . . and affectionate. She detached from Niamh immediately but it was too late.

Niamh raised her hand and stared at it in surprise. The blood smeared away from barely a crease on her palm. The wound was gone. Healed.

The damage was done.

# 10

'Sure, it was just a puncture wound!' babbled Niamh, washing the blood away under the tap. 'And there's me thinking I'd half chopped me hand off! Can't even see it now!'

Mary and Brigid peered at her healed hand while Mia stayed back, her shoulder blades pressed to the brick wall. She had quickly rinsed Niamh's blood off her own hands and was now doing everything she could think of to keep calm. Slow . . . steady . . . breathe. Smile. Smile in a concerned way. Now say something. *Say* something, you idiot!

'Sorry about the grabbing,' she said, with an attempt at a chuckle. 'I did first aid at college . . . thought it might need compressing, you know, to stop the bleeding. What a drama queen!'

'No, it was kind of you,' said Niamh, drying her

hand off with a bit of kitchen towel. 'And we can't have me bleeding all over the cake, now, can we?'

All three women smiled warmly at her. *Have they even* noticed *what the Effect was doing?* Mia wondered. Did they even question why they suddenly felt such a bond with her?

'So—what can I do to help around here?' she asked. 'I'm ready when you are!'

'Well—there's some sandwiches in need of making,' replied Mary. 'And then a bit of bath cleaning, if you don't mind. We'll show you how it all works. And Niamh can teach you to do the till if there's time today—it's not terribly cultural, mind!'

'Nonsense—seaweed baths are as ancient Irish as it gets,' argued Brigid.

The next two hours were spent learning how to set up each bath and clean it after use. Customers would book a half-hour slot in a bathing cubicle. The simple, whitewashed rooms were big enough for one roll-top tub, a chair, and a half-barrel for the seaweed. Brigid showed her how to run the baths at just the right temperature. The seaweed was kept in cold water in the barrel (delivered in batches from a very large tank which Donal kept filled from his daily harvest at the beach). When the bath was two-thirds full and steaming away, it was dropped in.

As soon as it hit the hot water the seaweed began to give up its bounty of luxurious gel, turning the water to liquid silk and giving off a rich mineral scent, just as it had the day before when Mia had slid into the bath at Brigid and Donal's cottage.

When the customer had vacated it was time to scoop out the used seaweed and let out the bath water and thoroughly clean the area before the process was repeated all over again.

It was quite tiring but Mia enjoyed it. The constant running and draining of water and the slip and slide of the seaweed soothed the part of her mind which kept threatening to uncover memories she didn't want. The gentle chit-chat with the women in the café in between her duties had a similar effect. Distraction. Fantastic distraction. She never wanted it to end.

'Are you sure you're OK?' asked Brigid, after Mia had cleaned out and re-run a third bath. 'I don't want to be tiring you out after all you've been through.'

'I'm fine!' smiled Mia, carrying in fresh towels. 'It's fun. I like it.'

Brigid smiled back. 'Well . . . just don't overdo it. You can come in and mind the till in a little while—that's a bit less physical.'

Learning the till wasn't difficult and the company of Mary and Niamh was very comfortable. It was busy but there was time for a cup of tea and some lemon cake between customers. Everybody seemed friendly and relaxed. Even more so as Mia passed them their change. Women smiled warmly at her and suddenly told her what a tonic their bath was . . . they really were feeling SO much better. Men—young and old—gazed at her for many seconds before collecting themselves.

Mia had to keep reminding herself of the Effect. She was doing it *again*—without realizing it. She was healing people. At its lightest touch, she was just giving everyone a dose of feel good. But here and there she knew she'd healed properly because she could feel their aches and pains echoing through her own body for a few seconds each time. That last man had arrived with dreadful sinusitis. Now it was gone and he'd left with a clear head and a full heart. She gulped, feeling the rattle and crunch in her own sinuses as the ghost of the departed ailment passed through her. She MUST back off.

This was trouble. She needed her . . . what? What did she need?

Black. It was something black. *Obsidian. Tourmaline.* She had used those crystals, hadn't she? To help control and block off her Cola power. Cola? What did that mean . . . Cola? Mia glanced at the cans of Coke and wondered if her mind was just sliding. But . . . no . . . C-O-L-A . . . it meant something.

'A penny for them, Maria,' said Mary, reaching past her for some cutlery. 'How're you doin' with that auld till? I think it's genuinely a museum piece—probably worth more than what's in it!'

Mia smiled down at the till which *was* an old mechanical one—not electronic. 'It's fine,' she said. 'I like it. I like it here.'

'Good—it's nice having you around,' beamed Niamh. 'Stay! Abandon your shallow college life and all pursuit of education and wrangle cake and seaweed instead!' She laughed but Mia knew her words were being driven by the Effect. She must get obsidian or tourmaline as soon as possible and block it. They often sold crystals in holiday gift shops, alongside the shells, didn't they? Maybe she could find some at Brannigan Beach.

The café door opened and a tall, slim woman with dark hair came in, holding a little girl by the hand. 'Niamh!' she called, looking theatrically wretched. 'Could you possibly, *possibly* help me out and mind Nell for me? Just for an hour . . . ?'

'Help *you* out?' replied Niamh, her hands on her hips. 'I need Nell to help *me* out! Look at the place!' She indicated the half-filled room. 'Not nearly enough people to eat all the buns.'

The little girl giggled, hanging off her mother's hand. She had thick dark hair, cut into a choppy shoulder-length bob and huge, liquid-brown eyes fringed with long sooty lashes. Her skin was milky and smooth and her small mouth pink. She was a beautiful child, thought Mia. Why was her mother so worried about her?

Mia couldn't read minds . . . but she sensed illness and emotional imbalance instinctively and she knew immediately that there was a worry about Nell, shared by all these women. What?

*Stop it!* she told herself again. *You MUST stop it. If you carry on like this you will have to leave this place soon. Sooner than you want to.*

Nell wandered across to Niamh and took her hand. 'Will you sit up at the till next to Maria?'

asked Niamh. 'She's new here so you can look after her.'

Nell nodded up at Niamh and, as her mother departed with promises to be back before closing, a high stool was brought across from the bar by the window, so she could sit up and see over the counter.

'Hello, Nell,' said Mia, smiling.

The little girl smiled back.

'How old are you?' asked Mia.

'Ah, she's nearly five,' said Niamh, wiping trays behind them. 'She doesn't talk though, Maria. Doesn't bother with such nonsense, do you, chick?' Niamh stroked the girl's head. 'Well, not so far anyway. And with all the women around her blathering away non-stop it's probably just as well.'

So that was it. Mia rested her hand lightly on the little girl's shoulder, which smelled of clean cotton and sugar paper. 'The world talks enough,' she said. Nell gazed up at her. She seemed to agree. She took Mia's hand and squeezed it.

Something in Mia's heart trembled.

'Here you go,' said Niamh, passing over some crayons and some paper napkins. 'We need some art, Nell. Pictures! Quick as you like!' She winked at the little girl and Nell let go of Mia's hand to turn to the crayons and napkins.

Mia was glad to let go. She didn't know why. She served customers, trying hard to reign in the Effect; avoiding too much eye contact. Only half an hour to go until closing time and she could get back to the cottage and try to work out what to do next. Where to go. How to get away from people.

'Aah, that's grand, Nell,' said Mary, pausing in wiping down tables to steal a glance at the little girl's pictures.

'Is that me?' asked Mary. Nell nodded. 'And Niamh, with all the hair! Sure, she looks like a film star! And that's Maria, is it? I love her dress! Like a dahlia! You've put her in a big orange dahlia dress. Niamh—she's going to be a fashion designer, this one!'

As Niamh came to look Mia gripped the edge of the till and felt herself go cold. She could see all Nell's pictures—smiley faces, curly hair, hands like spuds with stick fingers. It was clear who was who, but Mary had made a mistake about the picture of 'Maria'.

Nell shook her head at Mary and glanced back at Mia. And Mia met her eyes, understanding something which sent cold chills from her throat to her belly. Nell had *not* drawn her in a big orange dahlia dress.

Nell had drawn her engulfed in flames.

# 11

Pyrokinetic. That was the word. Nobody had said it out loud yet at Fenton Lodge and Chambers wasn't looking forward to being the first.

When the Children Of Limitless Ability were first discovered nearly five years ago there had been awe and amazement, disbelief, and then, of course, panic. As the government's go-to man for allegedly paranormal and extraterrestrial cases, Chambers had been brought in almost immediately to create the COLA Project. It fell to him to find the best location for the first college; to recruit teachers and mentors, some with enough paranormal talent to guide the youngsters who were already beginning to outshine them. He had hand-picked operatives like Owen Hind and tutors like Tyrone Lewis to guard and nurture his unpredictable charges.

It had never been plain sailing. It was fraught with danger and some of Chambers' choices had been badly wrong. One of them had cost Owen Hind his life; something that ate at Chambers to this day.

But how could *anyone* handle this? There was no handbook on how to successfully manage more than one hundred children who had suddenly developed ground-breaking paranormal talents. How could it ever—realistically—be contained? The clue to the problem lay in the *name*. Children Of *Limitless* Ability. Nobody knew where this was going.

How could you look after, educate, and nurture children who might one day be able to destroy you with the blink of an eye? Of course back then he, like everyone else, had thought the telekinetics were the biggest problem. Gideon and Luke Reader now had such phenomenal mind power they could hold back falling cliffs, and yet, with their decent and dependable natures, the twin brothers had proved to be the least of his worries. Other telekinetics seemed to share their characteristics—steady and loyal in their temperament, like Labrador dogs. It helped convince the government that teles were going to be a huge asset to the country—not a liability.

The glamourists were a mixed bunch. Those who could make themselves invisible were also going to be amazingly helpful and, as it turned out, very easy to handle. You didn't even need to be high-tech. A squirt of spray paint could identify them. Their talent was brilliantly useful but not seriously threatening. The illusionists were harder to predict. Darren Tyler was a pleasant young man, but easily led. The others didn't trouble Chambers yet—many of them were not *that* powerful. Spook Williams, though . . . Chambers sighed and shook his head. Soon he must go down to the containment levels and try to work out Spook Williams all over again.

The psychics, mediums, and dowsers were so far not a problem, he comforted himself. Phenomenally useful but rarely dangerous, with the possible exception of Lisa Hardman on a bad day. Chambers smiled to himself and then thought of the list and felt the smile slide off his face. What else then? Alex and Jacob Teller—the mimics. Good boys. Decent. And yet Jacob's talent had brought Chambers to his knees just weeks ago. It was not Jacob's doing; he had been used by Marcus

Croft. With his brother's life on the line, Jacob had had no choice.

The healers, surely, were nothing but good news, yes? None of them showed any sign of going the way Mia had.

What it all added up to was the same, though—phenomenal power at the UK's disposal. And phenomenal potential for disaster. Add in a rogue teleporter . . . *if* he was still alive . . . and it was nightmarish.

But if there was one thing that could ratchet disaster and nightmare up to catastrophe, he had just found it. A healer who wasn't just a healer.

A pyrokinetic.

A fire starter.

The Fenton Lodge estate was one large country house set in acres of remote Cumbrian fells. A low-level extension had recently been added to house most of the students and the teaching, catering, and medical staff. A further low-level complex in the grounds behind the house was where the scientists and the government staff worked. Closer to the perimeter of the estate were buildings where the military protection personnel worked and lived.

Below the government and scientists' block, however, was a network of chambers and corridors with a much bigger footprint. In one of these areas was Containment. Its subterranean walls were lead lined and threaded with black tourmaline and other minerals thought to protect against psychic attack, and more recently studded with magnetite—a protection against unwanted teleportation. *We're nothing if not adaptable,* thought Chambers, wryly, as he strode from the lodge, heading for Containment.

Until this last week it had never been occupied. He guessed it had only ever been a matter of time, but it still hurt him more than he would ever tell that it had come to this; that one of their own was down there.

'Hello, Spook.' Chambers let himself in and went to the water cooler immediately as the air locks on the door sealed with a quiet hiss behind him. Spook Williams was lounging on a long brown leather sofa, wearing black jeans and a black sweatshirt, reading one of his magic magazines. Any other COLA would surely be bashing the hell out of the state-of-the-art games console linked up to the huge high-definition flat screen on the wall. But Spook was not any other COLA.

'Hello, Mr Chambers,' replied Spook, not even looking up. 'Come to waterboard me?'

'Don't be ridiculous, Spook,' said Chambers, after a gulp from his cup.

Spook looked up, one dark auburn eyebrow raised. 'No, of course,' he said, silkily. 'You'll have more sophisticated torture methods, won't you?'

'Spook, you're not going to be tortured,' muttered Chambers. 'Don't be an idiot.'

'But I *am* a prisoner,' countered Spook. 'That was easy enough, wasn't it? Not much of a leap between imprisoning a minor and torturing him, surely?'

Chambers sighed and sat on a black leather chair beside a glass-topped table. 'You're here for your own safety, Spook. With everything that's happened recently we can't risk you getting spirited away again.'

'So why isn't *everyone* down here then?' asked Spook, putting aside his magazine and getting out a pack of playing cards. He upended the box and the pack slid into his palm. Seconds later he was performing some impressive shuffles, spinning and flipping the pack from palm to palm, through the air. The cards looked as if they were threaded together with invisible cord, dancing in perfect choreography between the boy's slender, agile fingers.

'You've really been practising, haven't you?' marvelled Chambers. 'I mean—that's not illusion, is it?'

'No,' smirked Spook. The cards suddenly burst into flame and Chambers blinked in spite of his experience of this kind of thing. '*That* is an illusion,' went on Spook. The flames blew out and the deck landed in a long and perfectly curved semicircle around Spook's feet. Each surface bore an image of Chambers' marvelling face, glasses glinting, mouth slightly agape. 'And so is that,' added Spook. He leaned forward and swept up the cards with aplomb, twisting them into a perfect fan. 'And that isn't. Still with me?'

'You are brilliant,' acknowledged Chambers. 'Quite brilliant.'

Spook snapped the cards together and returned them to the box. Then he sat back on the sofa, resting his hands behind his head in an apparently casual manner—although Chambers noticed he was careful not to mess up his exquisitely sculpted dark-red hair. 'So, *Mr* Chambers. What do you want today?'

'What I always want,' said Chambers. 'For you to tell me what's going on with you, Spook. And what happened with Mia.'

Spook laughed. 'But I *have* told you—everything I know. Even the mind readers can't dig out any more! I've been read and dowsed and hypnotized and . . . well, you know. All of it. I can't tell you any more, Mr Chambers, because there *is* no more.'

Chambers leaned across the table and fixed his gaze on the boy's strange amber-coloured eyes. 'And yet we both know that's not true, don't we, Spook?'

Spook said nothing but he shrugged and smiled ruefully.

'How *is* Lisa?' he asked, after a pause. 'It's not the same without her, you know. None of the other mind readers are anything like as rude and arrogant. I kind of miss it.'

'Do you really care?' asked Chambers. He had interviewed many a psychopath in his time and was occasionally tempted to believe that Spook was just one more. But that was lazy thinking. Spook was much, much more than that.

'Of course I care,' protested Spook. 'We COLAs must look out for each other. All for one and one for all . . . no doubt there's a whole gang of them outside this complex, waving banners about getting me released.' He laughed mirthlessly.

'You know what *happened* to Lisa, don't you?' asked Chambers, his face hardening. 'You were there. You saw it all, didn't you?'

Spook's face went peculiarly blank. 'I really can't remember,' he said.

And Chambers knew that when the mind readers came in again, Spook would seem to be telling the truth. 'Do you remember *him* yet?' he asked, plucking a photograph of a white-haired man from his pocket and handing it to Spook.

'Well, yes—I remember *him*!' Spook beamed. 'He's the man in the picture you've been showing me every day for the past month! He's "Important Picture Man", isn't he? Wish I could help further . . .' He shrugged.

'He's not good news, Spook,' said Chambers. 'Whatever he may have told you . . . however he *got* to you . . . Marcus Croft is very *bad* news. Trust me on that.'

'Whatever you say,' replied Spook, his eyes wide. 'I can't argue—if I ever met him, I really don't remember him.'

'When you *do* remember him,' Chambers said, quietly, 'and when you remember what you did to Mia . . . ' he noted, with small satisfaction, a flicker across Spook's smooth mask of indifference, ' . . . you will want to talk. And I will want to listen. And then we can both work out how we all carry on together.' He stood, walked over and touched the boy's shoulder. 'I don't want to lose you, Spook.'

He left the room.

In the observation booth two techies sat by their monitors. They glanced up as Chambers entered. 'Anything at all?' he asked and the man closest to him—Thompson—scratched his curly brown hair and yawned.

'Sorry, sir,' he muttered, noticing Chambers' raised eyebrow. 'It's been a long shift. Do you want to see the playback of the last session with Williams?'

'I do,' said Chambers.

'I wish I could tell you something exciting happened,' went on Thompson, pulling up a feed of Spook in a session with the principal and three mind-reading COLAs earlier that day. 'But it's much the same as every other time. Sartre brings in the group; they all gather round and do the relaxation thing . . . Williams seems to positively *enjoy* it. And then they rummage about in his head for half an hour and come away with . . . nothing. I mean . . . really nothing. Because you'd think *something* would be going on in there, wouldn't you? Even if it was nothing helpful.'

'It's like he gets the cleaners in just before they arrive,' commented Swift, the other techie, taking a sip of coffee.

On the screen Spook smiled serenely as the mind-reading team arrived; Jessica Moorland, Chloe Saville, and Matthew Gardner. These COLAs were what remained of Paulina's top group. Spook seemed to find the whole thing quite amusing, grinning and comically pressing his temples and blinking before settling back and submitting.

Chambers sat down suddenly, on a spare chair. 'Swift,' he said. 'What did you just say?'

'Um . . . sir?' Swift looked confused.

'What did you say about Williams?' prodded Chambers.

'Er . . . ' Swift wrinkled his brow. 'That he . . . that it was like he'd got the cleaners in . . . I think.'

'That's right,' agreed Chambers. 'Thompson.

83

Pull up the last six sessions. I want to see the start of all of them.'

Thompson's fingers chittered across his keyboard and the recorded sessions popped up across the screen in six small windows. He clicked PLAY on the first and Chambers leaned in, narrowing his eyes. He blinked, shook his head, and then reached over and clicked PAUSE on the first window, and then PLAY on the one next to it. Then the same for the next . . . and the next.

Thompson and Swift looked at each other. 'Can't believe we missed that,' said Thompson. 'Sorry.'

'Easy to miss.' Chambers stared at the freeze-frame of Spook in the latest recording. You couldn't see it in every one—sometimes one of the other COLAs blocked the view. But this one was clear. Fingers to his temples. Blink-blink-blink. The same thing in at least three of the sessions.

'It's his anchor,' Chambers said. '*And . . .* his tell. He's been taught how to self-hypnotize. To lock off his mind so thoroughly that not even Lisa Hardman could find anything.' He stood up, adrenalin coursing through him so fast he couldn't even work out which emotion it was serving—anger, excitement, betrayal? He pulled the photo from his pocket and flicked it in his fingers, fighting the urge to crush it in his fist. 'I know only one person who could teach a mind lock that good.'

He smiled grimly.

'No further contact with Williams. None at all. He's to be left alone until tomorrow when we will have another mind-reading session. And this time, no temple press and blink-blink-blink. No clean up. This time Spook's mind is going to be as messy as it should be. Nobody goes in before me. Is that clear?'

The techies nodded, but one added: 'Um— sir— could we do it sooner?'

'No,' said Chambers. 'It'll be several hours before his mind unlocks again. We go in now, we'll get nothing at all. He doesn't always do the tap and blink thing. I bet we'll find that on days when they've gone in to work on him more than once he's not done it later. No need. Mind still locked off. Check the feeds and tell me if I'm wrong. But by tomorrow I think Spook William's memory will be nicely back in play.'

He stared at the image of the illusionist on the screen, now reading his magic magazine again.

'Tomorrow, Spook,' he muttered. 'Before you know what's hit you.'

# 12

Mia was glad when Donal drove them back at six o'clock. The last half an hour with Nell had been . . . frightening. The girl kept looking at her. She *knew*.

And it was all Mia could do not to grab her, run down to the water's edge, stand her on the wet sand, and beg, 'WHAT do you know? What IS IT? What have I DONE?'

Mia couldn't read minds—but she read moods and ailments, of course. She could sometimes see auras around people, but mostly her reading of people's health, physical or emotional, was completely instinctive. She knew that Nell had no physical problem to stop her talking. Now she was sure it was a psychic thing. Nell had some talent. Nothing like on the COLA scale but still . . . talent.

And it was occupying her thought processes so much that at this stage in her young life, she simply didn't see the *need* to talk. Once she was full-time at school she would gradually start, Mia guessed.

Nell had solemnly handed each of them their crayon portraits when her mum dropped back in to collect her. Mia unfolded the paper napkin now and stared at it. Close up, she could see that it wasn't just the 'big orange dahlia dress' that Nell had done, its flames engulfing Mia's lower half. There were also little flames bursting out between Mia's spiky fingers. And worse—a wide crayon smile on her face.

That flare—*the crackle; the smell of burning hair*—went off in her head again and she had to stop herself crying out. It was coming back. Her memory was returning; she knew it. And she *needed* to have it back—she had to *know*. Except . . . she desperately, *desperately* didn't *want* to know. Because it was something horrific. And her fault.

'Here we are then,' called back Donal as they bumped along the track to the cottage. 'Well ready for our tea! Are you hungry, Maria?'

'Um . . . yes.' Her voice sounded normal. 'Yes, I am.'

'Good, because I put a pie on before I came to get you,' said Donal, parking the car and switching off the engine.

'Holy Mary, mother of God!' exclaimed Brigid. 'You remembered, for a wonder! You must visit more often, Maria. You keep him on his toes, so you do. Did you put the potatoes on too, auld man?'

'I did, you snippy auld baggage,' came back his fond reply. 'And the carrots too!' He pulled the handbrake on and winced with the sharp movement. The grimace vanished in an instant— he'd been burying his reactions to pain for so long now it was habit. Mia knew that sometimes he couldn't sleep through it—but suspected even Brigid didn't know this. She was certain, too, that he never told Brigid how gathering her seaweed was getting more agonizing with each day that passed. He loved her *that much*.

As they got out of the car, Mia's throat felt tight with emotion. She couldn't stop herself. She was going to have to do this. She stepped up beside Donal as they made their way down the uneven steps to the cottage, and took his left hand in hers. He drew a surprised breath, but didn't disengage. She'd known he wouldn't. Nobody ever did.

Instead he glanced across at her, fascinated. She smiled back and sent the healing. The tingle that ran from her skin into his seemed to swoop and turn and fall and rise like water in a whirlpool. The sharp hot spikes of his pain which jabbed through her joints from knuckles and wrists to shoulders, hips, and knees, made her eyes water.

*Not too much!* she tried to tell herself. *Not a miracle. A miracle will be SO hard to explain . . . just a little.* And she detached herself before Brigid could turn around and see the dazed look on her husband's face. Even so, she'd done too much. Donal's knuckles were visibly less swollen. Overnight the very calcium beneath the skin would soften and dissipate, smoothing the lumps.

Donal was silent as they walked down into the cottage. He glanced at her once or twice and seemed to be about to speak, but then he just shook his head and walked on. In the kitchen Brigid was taking off her coat and opening the oven simultaneously. 'Ah—you've managed not to burn it!' she chuckled. 'Will wonders never cease?'

The kitchen was filled with the comforting aroma of chicken and bacon pie and boiling potatoes and carrots. Mia helped make gravy and bring the meal to the table. Soon they were sitting, cutlery in hand, fragrant steam rising to their faces.

'Will I say grace?' asked Donal.

Brigid blinked. '*Will* you? It's not something you usually say. Are you on best behaviour for our Maria, then?'

'I just feel . . . blessed today,' said Donal, looking a little abashed as he glanced across at their guest. 'It's been a good day.'

'Then grace away!' chuckled Brigid.

Donal muttered, 'For what we are about to eat, and the special gifts we don't expect, we thank you, Father.'

Brigid gave him another searching look and then added, 'Amen.'

'Tuck in then!' grinned Donal, and they all did.

'Did we tire you out today, then, Maria?' asked Brigid, as they ate.

'Yes,' said Mia. 'But in a good way. I love your bathhouse. Will you take me again tomorrow?'

'If you like,' said Brigid. There was a pause, and Mia knew what was coming next. 'You seem so much better now. Is there a chance any of your memory has come back?'

Mia shrugged non-committally. What could she

say? *Yes . . . some of it's coming back. Will you please help me barricade my mind?*

'I don't want to push you,' said Brigid. 'But I can't help but think of how I would feel if you were my girl . . . my daughter or sister or niece . . . and I'd lost you. I feel terrible inside at the idea of your family so very worried.'

'I have no family,' said Mia.

'And you're quite sure of that?' went on Brigid. 'Nobody at all who cares for you? Who loves you?'

Another flash. Amber eyes. *Was that love?*

A fox. A falcon. A blonde-haired girl, running.

A man lying in a bed. Dark shadows under his eyes. Shallow breathing.

'I—I don't,' Mia dropped her knife and fork with a clatter and put both hands over her face. 'I can't!'

For a few seconds there was silence, and then she heard a chair scrape back and felt Brigid squeeze her shoulders. 'I'm sorry, chick, I didn't mean to upset you. C'mon—take a deep breath. You don't have to think about it now.'

Mia took a long, steadying breath and opened her eyes. 'I'm sorry,' she said. 'I think it's starting to come back . . . and then it goes again.'

'Well, there's no hurry,' said Brigid, smoothing

Mia's hair and then moving away, back around to her seat. 'Let's eat and talk about other things. If you chase a memory it runs away. You have to pretend you're not looking!'

'OK,' said Mia. 'I'm not looking.'

'Grand—then it'll pop up and surprise you like your best friend,' said Brigid.

'Like my best friend,' murmured Mia.

# 13

'Does she know we're here?' Chambers settled on a chair beside the bed.

Paulina Sartre shook her head from the chair opposite. She was an elegant Frenchwoman in her fifties, always beautifully turned out. Her light auburn hair was styled in a soft pleat at the nape of her neck, her grey eyes sad behind her spectacles. 'I don't think so. I can't reach her.' She sighed. 'I'm not good enough for this, David.'

'We're none of us good enough,' said Chambers, his eyes roaming unhappily across the bandaged arms of the girl in the bed; the drip feeding fluids into her veins. Her face—at least—was unmarked, but her once glorious long blonde hair was now raggedly short and still blackened in places.

'Will she live?' he asked.

Dr Jane Bell, known to the COLAs as Janey, picked up the chart at the end of the girl's bed. 'There's no reason why she *shouldn't* live,' she said, swiping her long dark hair off her face as she stared at the notes on the clipboard. 'Her lungs are healing nicely—they were never badly damaged to start with. The skin burns . . . they ought to heal over time, especially with COLA help. Of course, we don't have Mi—' She broke off abruptly, aware of blundering, and then continued more carefully. 'The concussion *was* serious . . . but there's no swelling in her brain now. It's what's going on in her *mind* I can't speak for. These aren't normal kids, are they? We can scan them and chart them and say what we like, but we don't know, do we? We don't ever really know what's going on in the COLA mind.'

'Lisa Hardman,' Chambers stood up, pushing the chair impatiently aside with a violent screech on the tiles, 'is one of the toughest COLAs we have. I cannot believe she isn't going to come out of this. We need to try some other healers. Psychics! Dowsers! *Somebody's* got to be able to get in there and find her!' He jabbed at the cropped head of the comatose girl. 'I will NOT LET HER stay in some vegetative state! Have you tried her dad again?'

'Endlessly,' sighed Paulina. 'Poor man. He can't get any response. He's gone back to the fell cottage to sleep now. He was exhausted.'

'Then—her friends! Who else? Who do we still have?'

'Dax Jones is gone,' sighed Paulina. 'But, David—I don't believe he's dead.'

Chambers rubbed his hands through his hair and shook his head. 'I *saw* the flames, Paulina. Dax was quick . . . but not quick enough.'

'No! He is NOT dead. I know this. He's . . . far away. But not dead. If we could bring him back I believe he could reach her. They've always had a special bond.'

Chambers laid a hand on Paulina's shoulder. 'I have the utmost respect for your talents,' he said, his voice gentle. 'But I know how much you care about these children. I *know* because I feel the same. And we must both understand that *wanting* something to be so . . . doesn't make it so.'

Paulina's eyes glittered. She said nothing.

'Her other close friends were Gideon and Luke,' said Janey. She shrugged, sadly. 'Sorry. Not much help.' She glanced further along to a side room where a man could be seen, his head bowed, his face obscured by the patterned glass in the door. There was no need to see his face to know the expression on it. Michael Reader was in a terrible state.

'Any news there?' asked Chambers, with a heavy heart.

'No,' said Janey. 'But we're not giving up.'

He didn't want to see them. Not again. But he got to his feet, knowing he must at least try to say *something* to their father. Michael Reader glanced up at him as he entered. There was hostility in his eyes. Chambers didn't blame him.

Gideon and Luke Reader lay side by side in their beds, attached to drips. One fair, one dark— but otherwise identical. Their burns were better, thanks to Janey's conventional treatment coupled with the attentions of COLA healers over the past two days. The COLAs had worked in groups, in shifts, almost continuously for the first twenty-four hours—and their efforts had not been in vain. The Reader twins and Lisa would never have survived without them.

But there was a long way to go. Something more than flames had struck them—something terrifyingly damaging—too much for the weaker COLA healers to handle.

'Have you found Mia?' asked Michael Reader. He looked as if he'd aged ten years in three days.

'We will,' promised Chambers.

'I can't believe this,' muttered Michael, anchored miserably between his silent sons.

'None of us can,' said Chambers. 'None of us knew.'

'Someone knew,' said Michael. 'Somebody *had* to have known.'

'Possibly,' said Chambers, thinking of the photo in his pocket. 'We'll find out.'

# 14

'What do you think?' asked Owen. He and Dax and Tyrone were sitting on the roof of the house. The roof wasn't tiles or thatch. It was a large chunk of mountain. The occasional thin plume of smoke might reveal that a chimney had been carved through from a dwelling inside the rock but the smoke escapes were convoluted and often expelled their telltale signs quite some distance from the homes they served.

'It's amazing,' said Dax. 'Perfect.' The rising sun threw rosy shafts of light across a tapestry of mountains and valleys in seams of brown, gold, green, and ochre. In the far distance the sea glowed silver on the horizon. Owen's house was deep in caves found in one of the higher passes, excavated over centuries. Dax couldn't believe how far it stretched—room after room; some lit and painted and some really still just caves. There were passages too, which led to distant exits more than a mile away from the main house, Tyrone told him. 'It's the coolest place to live I've ever seen!' marvelled Dax.

'We've done it up a lot,' Owen said. 'It was pretty basic when we got here. But ideal in many ways. Under all that rock we're very, very hard to find . . . even by a dowser.'

'We've got a neighbour about five miles west and another one about six miles south,' said Ty. 'But we don't visit each other. We've met on the mountain paths from time to time. We just nod and say, "Hola," and go on. Remote—that's what we are.'

'So no post then,' grinned Dax.

'I pick up stuff in the town,' said Ty. 'The local post office holds it for me. Owen, obviously, doesn't get post—being as he's dead.'

Owen laughed quietly and nodded. As far as the British government knew, he'd drowned in the North Sea two years ago.

'How do you live—I mean . . . how do you make money?' asked Dax.

'Life insurance pay out,' said Owen. 'It was

pretty good. My sister got it, of course, upon my "death" . . . and usefully gave it all to Tyrone—her "late" brother's best mate. She visits occasionally.' He smiled. 'It paid for the cave house renovations. But we work too—fruit picking and olive harvesting, a bit of building work, carpentry. Also we teach English to a few local kids in town. It's all cash in hand. And we don't need that much. We hunt and trap most of our meat.'

'I wish I could stay here with you,' said Dax. 'I could . . . couldn't I? Just forget everything else . . .' He stared down at his feet and the sadness and trauma of the past few days swept across his face.

'I wish you could, Dax,' said Owen. 'But you won't. You're not the forgetting kind. You came here for a purpose.'

Dax nodded. 'It was few hours before I came to you. I was out of it, hidden in the woods. It took a while to come out of the shock, I guess. That evening I ended up on the roof of Fenton Lodge, over medical. I shifted to a fox, hidden behind a chimney stack, and listened for a long time. Long enough to hear that Lisa was . . . ' he gulped, ' . . . pretty much dead. And Luke and Gideon were in a really bad way. They brought in healers to help them but . . . they were in such pain . . . and they couldn't talk . . . ' His voice wobbled as he thought of Gideon, his best friend, scorched and blistered. Owen squeezed his shoulder. 'The *smell* was the worst thing. And of course everyone was going nuts about Mia. All of the dowsers were trying to find her—but none of them did, as far as I could tell.'

'We have to find her,' said Owen. 'I don't think anyone can save Lisa and Gideon and Luke *except* Mia. And if she can save *them* . . . we might be able to save *her*. So where could she have gone? She can't have just *vanished*.'

Dax stared at Owen. 'But that's the thing . . . she *could* have vanished. She could have been taken by Olu.'

'Olu?' Owen shook his head. 'Who's Olu?'

'New COLA,' said Dax. 'He's a teleporter. Last month he took Alex and Jacob Teller for twenty-four hours and teleported them all over the planet.'

Owen's eyes widened in amazement and concern. 'A teleporter? God alive!'

'And that's not the worst of it. Olu might be dead . . . and might not. He fell into the sea but no one knows for sure that he died.'

'There was no body?' asked Owen.

'Yes—a body. But no way to be certain it was Olu. They didn't have any dental records or DNA or stuff.'

'OK,' said Owen, slowly. 'So, *if* he's still alive, you think he could have teleported Mia out of Fenton Lodge . . . And the worst of it . . . ?'

'Olu was with this guy . . . he called him Granite,' said Dax. 'A sort of . . . father figure, I guess. Saved his life and then looked after him and . . . started using him. And this guy, it turns out, knows David Chambers. He got Olu to take Jacob and Alex so he could use them to get to Chambers . . . and Chambers knows Granite too, from way back. Only he knows him under a different name—Marcus—'

'Croft,' cut in Owen. He looked deeply worried. 'Marcus Croft.'

'*You* know him?' asked Dax.

'Oh yes,' said Owen.

'And . . . ?' Dax prodded, after the man continued to stare in silence across the mountains to the distant sea.

Owen looked grave. 'Dax. I really hope you're wrong. I hope this Olu is dead and Marcus is gone for good and there's some other explanation for Mia's disappearance . . . '

# 15

Mia awoke from a falling nightmare. She cried out and sprung up in bed, awake instantly but still remembering the dream. Except she knew it wasn't a dream. It was a memory.

She was in the air with a boy with dark skin and eyes; a boy who was laughing. The boy was holding her up—somewhere/nowhere—high in the atmosphere. And at first he'd been thrilled and excited as if he'd just won her as a prize. And then the rage had come out of her and he had burnt. Screamed. Let her fall.

The falling had lasted an eternity. She had always believed that people blacked out when they fell long distances. Not so. Her cheeks and eyelids were blown almost inside out as the force of the air ripped most of her clothes away. The clothes were burning anyway. He caught her, but only for a moment, snagging her up before losing her again with a shriek of pain. She was too hot to hold. The last thing she remembered was slamming into the sea . . . and then waking up under the concerned gaze of Donal O'Malley.

So . . . that's how she got here. Maybe she and the boy had been in an aeroplane. A parachute jump gone wrong? *Oh come on,* part of her mind chided. *As if!*

Mia got up and wandered across to the dressing table mirror. A strange girl looked back, wearing one of Brigid's old nightgowns. 'Who *are* you?' she hissed at the reflection. She dropped her gaze to her fingers, seeing Nell's drawing of tiny flames between spiky digits. 'And what did you *do*?'

It was early. Not yet six. The house was still. She tiptoed out of the bedroom, collecting the coat she'd worn yesterday from a peg in the hallway, shuffled into her boots without bothering about socks, and quietly let herself out of the cottage. The morning breeze was gentle; it looked like it might be sunny today. She walked out of the garden and along the clifftop. It was time to find out. While nobody else was watching . . . somewhere she could contain it . . . if it was true.

She found one of the many rocky outcrops that rose out of the grass and dropped to the far side of it, blocking the breeze and her view of the cottage. Below the cliffs the beach was empty. There were no early joggers or dog walkers on the clifftop.

Mia sat cross-legged and looked for a focus point. A small sprig of thistle a metre away. That would do. She stared at it. Nothing happened. She stared harder, feeling her heart rate pick up as she *willed* herself to make it happen. Nothing.

Then she thought of the dream. The sense of being held up in the atmosphere—against her will. The rage from the dream suddenly raced up through her belly and seemed to narrow, squeeze . . . and then jet out of her solar plexus towards the thistle.

There was a crack and a hiss.

The thistle was alight.

A few seconds later it was nothing but a black stick in a drift of ash and a bittersweet scent on the air.

'So,' breathed Mia. 'Now you know what you are.'

She got up, pulling the coat tighter around her.

'But what did you *do*?'

# 16

Spook slept well and woke early. There was something about locking down his mind for a few hours which really made for good quality slumber. The Collector (or, apparently, Granite or Marcus Croft... who knew?) had taught him a very powerful skill with the deep mind lock. Now, whenever Spook triggered the self-hypnosis, *nothing* could get in. It made for a strange series of awakenings, though.

Every morning Spook woke up following the mind lock, he had to process the whole experience of meeting The Collector... what had led up to that meeting... and the instructions he had been left with, all over again. The memories seemed to fall out of the open mind lock in a heap and it always took him a few minutes to sort through them and work out exactly where he was in the plan. How far along. How successful.

It was an emotional process—frightening and exhilarating by turns. But for the last few days, for the first time, Spook had felt something else emerge from the jumble of memories and emotions. Worry. Deep, acidic worry. About Mia. What if she *wasn't* with The Collector? What if his teleporting boy, Olu, (some rogue COLA, apparently, whom Spook had never met before) had failed to rescue Mia?

But he *must* have. Because nobody knew where Mia was. What other explanation could there be? If The Collector now had her, nobody *would* know, would they? He would have dealt with the tracker chips in her clothes in an instant and shielded her from psychic dowsing even sooner. Spook cursed himself for not getting his own magnetite out *before* he'd cut out Mia's. He'd screwed up. Olu would have been able to port them *both* away if he'd done that.

Spook showered and then dressed in the windowless Containment bedroom. He liked to think of himself as a creature of the shadows, but if he was honest, he missed the sun. How long would they keep him down here? Surely not for much longer. Soon his family would want to know what was going on. But then . . . Spook felt a rather cold thud in his heart . . . sometimes his family went as long as two weeks without getting in touch.

He took a deep breath as he checked his reflection in the mirror. He looked well enough— good even. He'd lost a little weight but he liked the slightly hollowed look under his cheekbones. It went well with his magician style, although Mia would probably worry . . . when he saw her next. He fought down another fizz of anxiety about Mia. No. He must stop fretting. He had followed The Collector's instructions to the letter. Mia was safe.

'First,' The Collector had said, his ice-blue eyes steadily fixed on Spook's and his voice soft and hypnotic. 'Separate her from the others. She needs to understand that she is different. That she doesn't fit with them. That she is . . . a loner . . . like you, Spook. Like you.'

It hadn't been easy, but he'd achieved that. Yes . . . he had definitely pulled her away from the little Dax, Lisa, and Gideon clique. The four of them had been so tight. Of course, the adventures of the past few years had helped to bond everyone.

There was even a time when Spook himself had felt . . . part of things. He'd even, grudgingly, begun to respect Dax Jones after what the pair of them had experienced—but that was just a side effect of the assorted traumas they'd all been through. Over time it had worn off—Jones was so irritating. The only people he had grown close to here were Darren, his illusionist friend and dorm-mate, and—of course—Mia. Lovely, healing, incredibly dangerous Mia.

At first he hadn't believed it when The Collector had told him what Mia truly was. A healer . . . yes . . . but that was just a sideshow. What she *really* was shocked Spook to the core. A pyrokinetic. A human flame-thrower of the most terrifying kind. She was a deadly weapon and she had no idea. Or did she?

The Collector said she had killed Catherine— Gideon and Luke's sister—two years ago. 'Be glad of it, Spook,' The Collector had said to him. 'She saved your life. She saved everyone's life. But nobody knew . . . well . . . I think Dax Jones knew. He was right there when it happened.'

If Dax knew, Spook bet Lisa knew too—and probably Gideon. Maybe even Luke.

'Mia will suffer,' said The Collector. 'Because the idiots running the COLA Project will have no idea how to deal with her. As soon as it gets out, and trust me, one day, it *will* get out, Mia will be in lockdown. Either permanently drugged or trapped in a fireproof prison . . . probably both. Do you want that for her?'

Spook remembered tears rolling down his face. He'd been hypnotized at the time and unable to stop himself. No. He didn't want that for her.

'I know how to look after her,' said The Collector. 'And I know how to *stop* her. And that is what she needs more than anything else, Spook. Someone who can stop her. Nobody can handle that kind of power until they know where the brakes are. I will show her where the brakes are—and teach her to apply them.'

Spook hoped Mia was already being taught. There was something both delicious and awful about the way he had manipulated her. He wanted to see her soon—to make sure she forgave him and still loved him. All he had to do now was get *out* of this bunker and into the open where The Collector could reach him; where this boy Olu could port in and get him out.

Well, as soon as he'd dealt with the magnetite . . .
Spook eyed the soft area on his right palm beneath
his thumb with an irritated sigh. He could just
about make out the shadow of the lozenge of black
magnetite under the skin. The Teller brothers had
found out that Olu could not port anybody while
they were in skin contact with this mineral—and
then everyone had to have it inserted in their
palms. He'd had to go along with it, knowing that,
when the time came, a little light surgery was going
to be necessary.

No matter. Soon they'd have to admit there was
nothing they could find in his head to help them,
and he'd be free again.

Freer than they were prepared for.

It was only 6 a.m. when Chambers came back but
Spook had been up and dressed for half an hour.
The lack of sunlight had affected his body rhythms,
he guessed. The man looked grey—he clearly
wasn't going to win this war of nerves.

Chambers was locked onto target; physically
and mentally prepared. Although he'd come to
care about the teenagers in his charge over the
past five years, he had never forgotten what they

were—COLAs. Not to be underestimated. He had maintained his personal fitness and field training rigorously for just such an occasion as this. And he had never let sentiment cloud his thinking.

Spook was sitting up at the glass-topped table. Good. He was already on the chair Chambers would have chosen for this. Chambers felt the plastic strips in his pocket and walked across to his target.

'Hello, Mr Chambers,' said Spook. 'Come for another friendly chat?'

'Indeed I have, Spook.'

Spook glanced up to see Chambers walking over to him with his hands in his pockets—obviously attempting the casual approach this time.

Spook found it all quite entertaining. Chambers was harmless when it came down to it. He might be the big bad boss of the COLA Project—right up there with the Prime Minister and the head of MI5, but what could he really *do*? Spook toyed with throwing a little fun illusion to wind the man up . . . but this might put Chambers into a bad mood and increase his sentence in lockdown. He'd better not.

Chambers stepped behind his chair and touched

him lightly on the shoulder. 'Remembered anything yet?' he asked.

'Sorry—no,' smiled Spook. And what happened next came so fast he had no idea exactly *how* it happened. One second he was relaxed, his elbows on the table, the next second his arms were violently jerked behind him and Chambers was tugging something plastic and vicious tightly around his wrists.

Spook shouted out in shock and protest. He couldn't believe it was happening. Now Chambers was yanking his bound wrists back against the metal frame of the chair and attaching them firmly to it. Spook tried to pull away but the bindings on his wrists cut sharply into his skin.

His heart was suddenly thundering in his chest and there was a rushing sound of fast-pulsing blood in his ears.

'What are you *doing*?' he yelled, panic making his voice high-pitched. He tried to stand up but Chambers seized his shoulders and slammed him and the chair down so hard his teeth rattled.

'Stay put, Spook,' he ordered, in a flat cold voice. 'You're going nowhere.'

At this point the door opened and two men he

did not recognize came in. One was carrying some black material, folded over one arm. The other held a small silver case. Spook's throat constricted with fear. He had joked about torture. It seemed a whole lot less funny all of a sudden.

In his panic he sent snakes. In a moment the floor was a seething mass of hooded cobras, garter snakes, black mambas, rattlers, huge yellow anacondas—anything his scared imagination could pluck out and throw. They hissed and rattled and spat venom at the two men, who froze by the door, their faces a mask of shock.

'It's an illusion,' said Chambers, calmly, from behind his chair. 'Keep moving. We need the hood so we can stop all this nonsense. He can't keep it going without a sight-line.'

The men each took a deep breath and then walked through the snakes. They couldn't stop their pupils shrinking to tiny dots of fear or resist flinching as the snakes struck at them again and again.

It didn't stop them, though. The first man to reach him—a dark-haired guy with a flat, closed face—slid a thick black hood over his head. The last thing Spook saw was the other man, balding and stocky, opening the case on the table, revealing a set of syringes.

Spook's shout of protest died in his throat as a bizarre sensation hit his hands. Chambers, reaching in through the back of the chair, had pushed them into some kind of tub filled with a cold, porridgy substance. Spook shuddered and tried to pull them out but within three seconds the substance had set completely—like dense rubber. He was completely unable to move his fingers. This sent lightning strikes of panic through him—far more than the wrist binding.

'So . . . ' said Spook, his voice shaking and muffled under the hood. 'I was right. It's torture now, is it?'

Chambers gave a low chuckle. 'Tempting though it is, Spook . . . no. I don't think we need to inflict any pain today.'

Spook could have argued. Chambers' ruthless capture of his wrists had given him considerable pain. His shoulders were smarting still from the man's iron grip but his wrists were worse. He recognized the feel of plastic ties—the thin, bendy kind with sharp vinyl teeth which bit into the strip as it was tightened and would never give under pressure. The only way out of such ties was with sharp scissors. Tugging against them hurt. A lot. And the sensation of the hard rubber immobilizing his fingers was extremely unpleasant. What next? He remembered the syringes.

'Are you going to inject me with something?' he asked, trying hard to sound more aggressive than afraid. In fact he was terrified; feeling sick and horrifyingly in need of the toilet.

'We might,' said Chambers. His voice was mild and unhurried, as if he were a teacher about to start an interesting new topic with his class. 'But we'll try the usual route first. Bring them in.'

Spook heard the door open again, with a hiss of the pressure lock, and was aware of several people entering the room. They were silent but he heard a few gasps and guessed it was the usual group of mind-muggers he'd been dealing with for the past few weeks (minus Lisa, of course).

Then realization struck. It felt like a wrecking ball hitting his chest. He *could not* do a deep mind lock. Not without his anchor. He could not move his hands up to touch his temples before he blinked. He couldn't move his fingers *at all*. Chambers must *know*! His mind raced as he hitched in short, shallow breaths of panic. Any second now the psychics were going to be all over him, picking through his subconscious like locusts—and they MUST NOT get IN! They MUST NOT!

'Mrs Sartre!' he pleaded. 'Please—stop this! Don't let them torture me!'

'Nobody's going to torture you,' she said, her voice low but the upset in it clear to his ears even under the hood. 'I'm sorry it has to be like this, Spook, but it's for your own good. We know someone has programmed you . . . brainwashed you. This is the only way we can rescue you and find out what's happened to Mia. Please don't fight us.'

He heard whispering now and sensed the psychics moving closer. He tried to blink three times under the hood, hoping that the anchor might still work without his fingers pressed to his temples. It didn't. And the realization made him feel even more sick. 'Jessica! Matthew!' he yelled out, guessing these two would be among the group. The sharp intakes of breath he got back confirmed it. 'Don't DO this! Don't let them make you do it! They're hurting me! I'm a COLA like you! We have to look out for each other! You do this now and next time it'll be YOU in lockdown and maybe one of *your friends* will be helping them!'

He heard Jessica stifle a sob. 'We're not going to hurt you, Spook,' she sniffled. 'We need to find out what happened to you and make it better. Please . . . just let us in!'

Spook threw shutters in his head, the way he'd learned to years ago when he first met other COLAs who were psychic. It had been easy, back then, to keep them out—but now they were older and much more powerful. None of them a patch on Lisa Hardman, true, but still good enough to find out about—NO! He rejected the image of The Collector the second it flashed across his mind. Tried to replace it with . . . Miss Piggy from The Muppets.

'There's a man,' said Matthew. 'He has white hair and really blue eyes.'

Spook let out a howl of rage and then went super-quiet and super-still, focusing on a thick, thick concrete barrier. They would NOT get in! They would NOT!

'He's blocking us now,' said Jessica.

'Yes,' said Chambers. 'He will. But it's just a question of how long he can keep it up. When he gets tired it'll fail and you'll get in.'

'He's strong,' said Matthew. 'It could be a long time.'

'Let's speed up the process a little,' said Chambers. Spook felt his sleeve being tugged up his right arm. He gave a shout of rage and horror as he felt the needle slip into his vein, pushing in a jet of something cold which rose up his arm and spread across his chest in seconds.

Suddenly he felt incredibly tired. He focused hard on the thick concrete barrier across his psyche but holding it in place was getting harder and harder, as if the weight of it were crushing him. His body slumped forward in the chair. He was too tired even to cry out at the bitter pain from the cheese-wire bindings around his wrists. He could sense the mind-muggers getting in.

*Get OUT! I'll pay you back for this!* he bawled, inside his burgled brain, but they were well past his barriers now, foraging deep, deep into his memories and plans.

'We're in,' Jessica told Chambers, in a thin, strained voice. 'Oh God . . . '

# 17

Donal woke up with wonder. He raised his hands above the quilt and stared at them in the morning light. He flexed his fingers and watched them move . . . easily . . . without pain.

'It's a miracle,' he murmured.

How far had the miracle spread? Any ordinary morning it took five minutes to get out of bed, the ache and burn spreading slowly through his stiff joints. Today, though, he stood up in ten seconds. He walked to the window and peered outside. It was a bright morning and the sea was a promising shade of mauve, but Donal barely saw it. He was in a state of shock. *Where* was the pain? Where had it gone? He stared again at his fingers; it wasn't just that they could move properly, for the first time in five or six years, they *looked* better too—

the lumpy, gnarled knuckles were smoothed out. Not to complete perfection—but enough that few people would guess he suffered from arthritis. If he still did.

Donal dressed—with ease—and drifted into the kitchen. Maybe somebody had slipped some kind of opiate into his food. They said that about morphine and the like, didn't they? It took away the pain and made you feel as if you were floating . . . He eyed his packet of Voltarol tablets on the shelf, tucked behind the tea caddy. These had never made him feel high. In recent months they'd done precious little to stop the pain, either. Behind them sat a shiny blue packet of Prednisolone—steroids he'd been prescribed a year ago. He'd not taken any yet, worried about the side effects. Only last week he'd been thinking, as he dragged his crop out of the sea and almost cried out with the pain, that he might have to give in to that little blue packet.

But today . . . today he didn't even feel the need for Voltarol. Or half a paracetamol! What was going on? Arthritis didn't go away, did it? If you were lucky it just got worse . . . slowly.

Donal made coffee, strong and sweet, and tried to put his fanciful notions out of his head. But it all came back to Maria. His pain had been sharp enough when he'd walked across the beach to find her . . . but since then he'd been getting steadily better and last night, when they were walking back down the path and she took his hand. The *warmth*! The *love*! It was like being touched by an angel.

He sat at the table, his hands around the hot mug, and felt the urge to weep. How had he come to deserve this?

'Didn't make one for *me*, then!' chided Brigid, padding past in her slippers and dressing gown. 'Well . . . *you* look perky!'

'Do I now?' he asked and she turned to stare at him.

'What is it?'

Donal put down the mug and spread his fingers across the tabletop.

'Holy mother of God!' Brigid whispered. 'What happened?'

He shook his head with a little smile. 'I have no idea! Watch!' And he lifted his hands up and flexed each of the fingers and thumbs. 'It doesn't hurt. And watch . . . ' Now he stood up and twisted left and right from his hips, then stood on one leg and raised his knee. 'No pain.'

'It's a miracle!' Brigid hugged him.

'So it is,' he agreed. 'When did I get so deserving? It's not like I've even been to Mass since last Christmas. Just what passing angel thought *Donal O'Malley* might be a worthy cause?'

Brigid looked at him and then glanced along the corridor to the closed door of the guest room. She looked back at her husband and he was nodding at her. 'I know,' he said. 'I know.'

When Mia got up, for the second time that morning, Donal was already off down the beach gathering seaweed and Brigid was making soda bread.

'Will I be working at the bathhouse again today?' she asked, brightly.

Brigid turned, smiling, and something in that smile sent a shard of panic through Mia. Brigid looked . . . grateful. Suffused with delight and wonder. Something had happened.

*Damn!* After her shocking discovery early that morning, she had forgotten her idiocy of the night before. She had healed Donal. In one stupid, thoughtless moment, she had given in to her healer's urge and taken his hand and . . . even then she had tried to stop herself, but obviously she'd been too late.

'It would be grand to have you along again, Maria. If you're sure you'd like to come,' said Brigid.

'I need to work off my debt to you,' said Mia, glancing down at her clothes. Today she had put on the cargo pants and the green top. 'You must have spent a hundred euros or more on all this.'

Brigid put the soda bread dough into the oven. 'No more than eighty,' she said. 'I've a good eye for a bargain. But if you work on for longer I can pay you—how would that be?'

'That would be fine—great,' said Mia. 'Maybe . . . after a week or so . . . we can talk again about, you know, people who might be looking for me.'

'That sounds like a very good plan,' said Brigid. 'I'm really pleased you're thinking that way. And in the meantime, it's lovely to have you around. You've really put a spring in Donal's step, so you have!'

*I have*, thought Mia, with a shiver. *I just hope that's all I've done.*

After her walk along the cliff that morning it had taken half an hour, back in her room, to get her racing heart under control. She was a pyrokinetic. Two sides of one coin—healer and destroyer. It had occurred to her that the best thing she could do might be to step off the cliff. End it all now. Because

124

she sensed that her memory was returning—and the horrific things she had done could engulf her at any second.

But surely she *must* have done good too. The healing power in her was very instinctive and practised—she knew she had helped many, many people. Maybe what had gone wrong wasn't *so* bad. Maybe the good she had done would outweigh it . . . ?

As her heartbeat gradually slowed and her breathing got steadier, she'd formulated a kind of plan. She must earn some money and get away from here. She didn't want to be around Brigid and Donal when her memory returned. She knew it would bring trouble and they did not deserve it, just for being kind to a stranger. She would get away somewhere . . . maybe to Dublin. Somewhere she would not stand out so much. She'd get some black obsidian and tourmaline too—and fill her clothes with it until it blocked out the Effect. She could become invisible, almost, if she kept her head down and stemmed the feel-good vibrations which flowed out of her to anyone passing.

She had toyed with the idea of stealing from the till at the bathhouse and running away that night—

but knew she couldn't bear to do that. No—she must earn. And do everything she could to hold off that returning memory until the end of the week when she might ask for some money.

Her second day at the bathhouse was much like the first. She absorbed herself in what she was doing and asked questions to get Niamh and Mary talking about their lives. Mary was married to a builder and had two grown up sons—one away on a gap year and the other starting his first job after university in Dublin. Niamh was married to a music teacher—they had no children, although they hoped to one day. Nell's mother, Sarah, was Niamh's best friend from England—an actress and a singer, married to an Irish architect. Nell was a regular visitor at the bathhouse.

Everyone seemed so involved in everyone else's lives, thought Mia. Was it possible *she* had known so much about the people in her old life? Before now? She kept thinking of a blonde girl . . . running . . . She wanted to see the girl's face . . . to know more . . .

*Don't,* a voice from somewhere dark inside her warned. *Wherever she is now, she's long gone from you.*

# 18

The medical wing was in one of the oldest parts of Fenton Lodge. In years gone by it had been servants' quarters—something which its low ceilings and dormer windows revealed to anyone who knew their architectural history.

There had been a house on this site for five hundred years but the current one was built in the eighteenth century, over the ruins of an older building. Many changes had been made to the building since then but the top floor had changed little. Several small rooms had been knocked through to make a long medical ward and Janey's office, but aside from the lost walls the layout was much the same.

In fact, if you knew where to look, you could find old plans of the original Georgian building and clearly see the layout of each floor as it had once been. There were photos, too, of the interior in 1943 when the house had been requisitioned as a military hospital. Again . . . you needed to know where to look.

Marcus Croft, aka The Collector, aka Granite, knew where to look.

'Is this enough?' he asked and Olu nodded. The boy sat on the window seat with the tall glass panes behind him framing grey sky over a distant headland. He scratched absently at the wounds across his arms, shoulders, and one side of his face. The attack had blistered his dark skin, burnt off some of his hair, and left him howling with pain for hours. Marcus had done what he could with his healing touch, but his energy levels were low and he thought the boy would probably always be scarred . . . unless his attacker could be found and persuaded to make good the damage.

'Good,' he told Olu now, patting him on his uninjured shoulder. 'Are you up to this? If you need more rest, just say.'

Olu had slept for two days. He'd been in shock as much as in pain. He had never lost anyone before. The girl had blown his circuits for a while. Marcus cursed her and marvelled at her by turns. It was rare that he was outmanoeuvred. This time he'd been thwarted because of random luck . . . although how lucky it had turned out for Mia was anyone's guess. Olu had no idea where she'd landed or if she'd survived. They badly needed to find out and there was only one person on this planet who might be able to help. *If* they could reach her.

'It's OK—I'm ready,' said Olu, determined not to seem weak. He'd had far worse pain than this when his old man used to beat him up back in Manchester, and then he'd been just a kid. He could handle it. And he wanted to make it up to Granite. He'd screwed up badly. Olu stared at the pictures again. They were black and white and grainy, but the floor plans helped—along with descriptions they'd got from Spook. Granite had collected a lot of detail from the illusionist about Fenton Lodge.

'If it goes wrong,' said Granite. 'Bring us back here. Don't wait to ask me—just do it. And we'll rethink.'

Olu gulped. He could teleport anywhere in the world—but he had to have seen it first. A photograph would do—but an old photograph? Seventy-odd years old? There could be new walls . . . suspended ceilings . . . raised floors. It was dangerous. He never materialized *in* something solid but would be thrown, powerfully, to the nearest space, if he got it wrong. He'd broken an arm that way once. The nearest space had been several metres up in thin air.

'What about the magnetite?' he asked, pausing before he took hold of Granite. Magnetite was the only thing that could stop him from teleporting . . . and he knew the COLA Project people were aware of this.

'Don't worry,' said Granite. 'We'll handle it.'

Olu grasped the man's arm and seconds later they were standing in a corridor, on thick green carpet; the top floor of Fenton Lodge. Granite turned and opened a door, pulling Olu into a linen cupboard. Inside he found a switch and a dim energy-saving light shone overhead. 'There are security cameras so put your hood up and only walk where you have to,' he said. 'Go one floor down, find room twelve. That's Darren Tyler's room. According to the timetable Spook furnished me with, he should be in his room studying before lunch. You'll need this.' He thrust a scalpel-sharp knife into Olu's hand.

'What for?' hissed Olu. 'To threaten him?'

'No—to cut out the magnetite. It'll be here.' Granite prodded the plump area of skin below Olu's right thumb. 'You should be able to see a dark shadow under the skin. You can get it out in seconds as long as you stay focused. He'll be shocked—you won't.'

Olu ported to the end of the corridor which he'd glimpsed before they entered the cupboard. From here he could see the lower landing. A second later he was on it. Then a long corridor off to his right. Another second and he was halfway down it, scanning the numbers. He found Room 12 with a glance and was at the door in a fraction of a second. The whole journey had taken less than four seconds. He went in. Darren Tyler—Spook's best friend—lay on his bed, snoozing, an open history book laid across his chest.

The bed next to his, on the far side of a tall window, was neatly made up and empty. A shame, thought Olu. How much easier it would have been if Spook had been allowed to stay in his own room. Granite had known he would be in lockdown.

Now they'd have to make do with Darren, who wasn't even half as powerful an illusionist. Still—

better than nothing. Olu glanced at the boy's right hand, flung out over the edge of the bed. Crouching close to it, he could see a small, dark oblong shape under the skin. He unsheathed the blade and gritted his teeth. This was going to be nasty—and risky. He didn't want Tyler screaming the place down. He prodded the boy with one finger. 'Wake up!' he said. 'Spook needs your help.'

'Wha-what?' burbled the boy, getting up on one elbow, his mousy hair squashed and his face creased with confusion as the book fell to the floor.

Olu grabbed his shoulder. 'Be quiet and don't make a fuss. I need to get this out so you can help your friend!'

And before Darren could say another word Olu sliced across the skin of his palm, directly over the dark shadow. Darren gasped with shock but it wasn't until the lozenge, dripping in blood, lay on the floor that the pain really hit. And by then his cry was muffled by the linen cupboard. Olu had ported him upstairs instantly.

Granite pulled the boy to his feet and spoke in his ear. 'Make a noise and Spook will never come back.' Darren glanced up at him and then bent over and vomited. 'I'm sorry Olu had to cut you,' went on Granite, grasping the boy's shoulder and steadying him. 'But we are here to help rescue Spook and he is *depending* on you to help—do you understand?'

Darren nodded, his face white and his grey eyes glassy. 'Darren—we need you to shield us with illusion as we walk out into the corridor,' explained Granite, grabbing a flannel from the shelving behind him and wrapping it tightly around the boy's bleeding hand. 'Nothing fancy—just some dark shadow will do. And you need to keep it up while we go into the medical room and see Lisa.'

'Lisa can't help you!' whispered the boy. 'She—she's in a coma!'

'Don't worry about that, just do as we say—do you understand?' said Granite. 'No harm will come to you . . . and Spook will never be able to thank you enough.'

'Fine—I'll do it,' grunted the boy. He was shaking, badly scared, but getting steadier as he pulled out of the disorientation of his first teleport.

'Good boy,' said Granite, and opened the door. They progressed along the corridor in silence. Darren's face was focused and set and Granite could sense that he was projecting the shield around them. The security cameras would see nothing unusual unless a guard was staring at them very, *very* intently. They might, of course, have spotted him and Olu porting in earlier and leaping into the cupboard, but he doubted it. It would be there on recordings if anyone looked later, but by then it would be too late. Granite knew that even for highly trained military guards it simply wasn't possible to stare at a bank of monitors non-stop for an entire shift and see everything.

The medical unit—a long, low-ceilinged room with four beds along one side and a separate glass-walled cubicle with two more beds at one end—was warm and quiet. To their right was the office area, partitioned off by more glass walls, where Dr Jane Bell worked. She was there now, her back to them and her head bowed over her desk, reading.

He and Olu, each holding one of Darren's arms, stepped over to the bed where Lisa Hardman lay.

*Shame about the hair,* thought Granite, seeing her picture in his mind—a beautiful girl with long, shining blonde hair. He guessed most of it had been burnt off; the blackened ends trimmed away.

He let go of Darren and Olu held onto the boy, stepping aside as Granite sat in the chair beside

Lisa's bed. Granite took a long, deep breath, marshalling his resources, and then took her hand in his. It was time to enter Lisa World.

The minute he stepped inside, Lisa punched him in the face.

# 19

Mia went for a walk in her lunch break. It was another bright day. The sea was choppy and lively, rushing in to meet the high cliffs which bordered the sandy bay and gurgling deep inside their many caves. The beach was busy with families. After twenty minutes of sea breeze in her face, Mia went into Bernie's Beachware & Gifts and saw, amid the hats, sunglasses, and flip-flops, a glass counter filled with minerals, rocks, fossils, and shells. She made a beeline for it and raked her eyes quickly through the crystals on offer; plenty of amethyst and rose quartz, along with Irish green marble cut into shamrock shapes. Then she spotted a rather dusty tray of black minerals towards the back of the display. They were hexagonal chunks, gently gleaming like coal. The marker on them read

'Black Obsidian'. Yes! Each piece was two euros. She'd need as much as she could get and it looked like there were around a dozen pieces. How could she get twenty-four euros, though, when she hadn't yet worked off the cost of the clothes?

She glanced around, wondering, for the first time in her life, whether she could shoplift. The shopkeeper was a nice looking plump lady—*Bernie?*—sitting at the counter by the door. She smiled across at Mia and returned her attention to her health magazine.

Mia wandered closer to her, checking out the magazine but also letting her senses pick up the woman's physical state. It was her feet. Yes . . . she'd felt a wave of the woman's discomfort as she'd arrived in the shop, but was so used to picking up random pain from strangers that she was adept at shoving it away with barely a thought. Now she let it back in again. The woman had swollen and painful feet. She got this a lot and was always seeking a remedy for it. The main cause was that she was overweight, eating unhealthily, and not getting enough exercise—it was causing circulation problems and she was only a month or two away from developing Type 2 diabetes.

'I'm always searching for remedies in health magazines, too,' said Mia, smiling sympathetically.

The woman looked up, the magazine open on her counter. 'I keep hoping!' she chuckled.

'Is it your feet?' asked Mia, glancing at an article entitled 'STEP OUT OF PAIN', thanking her lucky stars for such an easy in.

'They're a nightmare!' admitted the woman, swinging out two chubby feet in flip-flops. 'They ache night and day! Maybe I should get them chopped off and be done with it.'

Mia crouched down, sending waves of the Effect out so the woman would accept what she was about to do. 'I studied massage for a while,' she said. 'I bet I could take the edge off—shall I try?' And she laid her warm hands on the woman's feet.

Luckily the shop was empty, or she might have had a harder time of it, but the woman just let out a surprised gasp and then a sigh of delight as the healing flowed through her. Mia did some random massage, to at least give the impression that it was this which was giving such relief. After three minutes she stood up and the woman gaped at her in wonder. She got carefully onto her feet and walked a few steps.

'That is AMAZING!' she marvelled. 'How did you DO that?'

Mia shrugged. 'It's . . . technique . . . ' she said, rather lamely.

'That's the first time anything's worked!' gasped the woman. 'I don't know what to say! Thanks a million! You know, I think people would pay good money for that. You should set up a business. I'd come to you, for sure! What's your name? I'm Bernie...'

'Um – hi Bernie. I'm Maria. Do you think people *would* pay?' asked Mia, feeling a flush creep over her face as she got down to the *real* business.

'Hundreds!' said Bernie. 'I should pay you now! Would you like something for your trouble?'

'Oh no . . . at least . . . ' Mia eyed the minerals display. 'Unless you can spare some of that black obsidian you have there.'

Bernie ducked down behind the display and retrieved the tray. 'How much would you like?' she beamed. 'Happy feet make me feel very generous! I've some snowflake obsidian if you like—that's much prettier . . . '

'No, it's the black I need . . . ' said Mia. 'Um . . . maybe seven or eight . . . ' But the woman was

139

already tipping the entire contents of the tray into a thick paper bag.

'Here—have all of it. And it's a bargain for me. Let me know if you set up in business, will you, Maria? I'll be needing you when the pain comes back.'

'I will,' said Mia. She took the woman's hand and sent a different kind of healing in. 'But it won't come back . . . at least, not for a long time . . . if you sort out the exercise and the food. You know that—don't you?'

The woman's face grew pink and her eyes filled with tears. 'I do know it,' she breathed. 'At least . . . I know it *now*.'

'Good—then you'll do what the doctor says and make yourself better?'

'Yes!'

Mia left the gift shop with her package of black obsidian and some quite intense pain in her feet.

# 20

'I've been *waiting* for you,' Lisa said, her glossed upper lip curling as he got back onto his feet.

In her own mental landscape Lisa still had all her long hair. She was dressed in black drainpipe jeans, a pale blue, tight-fitting sweatshirt with the linked Cs of Coco Chanel glittering on the chest, and some spiky-heeled black leather boots. Her hair was in a high ponytail and her dark blue eyes were almost spitting fire, she was so angry.

'Glad to see your subconscious still wears the top labels,' remarked Marcus, wiping away the blood that dripped from his nose in Lisa's elaborate construct. 'Chanel's coma poster girl!'

She kicked him then, in the thigh, with the spiked heel of her boot. It hurt a lot. It made him first amazed and then angry. To be able to inflict pain on him in this universe she'd made from her own subconscious was something extraordinary—and upsetting. He needed to take back some control—make a few constructs himself. The contact he was making with her, back in the real world, was fuelling his 'collecting' talent—he reminded himself that he was very nearly as powerful at this business as Lisa herself was right now. He made a black leather armchair and sat in it.

'So, you were expecting me,' he said. 'You know who I am. That's flattering.'

'Don't kid yourself,' she sneered. 'You're just a jumped up little parasite like Catherine, nicking other people's talents.'

'You have to admit it's a useful skill,' said Marcus, resting his hands along the arms of the chair in a study of nonchalance. 'You're in a deep, deep coma. Possibly for good. None of your COLA classmates could reach you—not even Paulina Sartre could, nobody could, apart from a psychic of the same strength as you. And the minute I touched your poor burnt hand, that's what I became. So, let's not waste each other's time or energy. You know what I'm here for. Dowse Mia for me, there's a good girl.'

'Dowse her yourself if you're so skilled,' she replied.

'Aaah, I would. But I don't have the connection with her that you do . . . yet.'

'Ha!' she said, throwing back her head. 'So— bad luck, Marcus!'

Marcus conjured a mirror and shoved it at her. In it was her reflection . . . the real thing. A girl with burnt arms and scorched hair, lying like wreckage in a hospital bed.

'She didn't leave you looking too good, did she?' he jibed. 'Your so-called best friend . . . '

Lisa stood still and gazed at the image. Her face lost its defiance and crumpled as horror and despair seeped into it.

'She didn't do a great makeover on your friends, either,' said Marcus, flipping the mirror and showing her Gideon and Luke. 'And Dax Jones is spit-roast, I gather.'

Lisa slumped to the polished wood floor of her world. 'No . . . ' She began to cry.

He got out of the chair and moved towards her, softening his manner. 'Lisa—what have you got to lose? Help me find Mia and I will first make her put you and the Reader twins back together . . . and then take her away where she can't hurt you again.'

'Mia . . . ' sobbed Lisa. 'How could you do this?

We loved you . . . '

'You're weren't to know,' said Marcus. 'There is evil in all of us, but Mia's is . . . so much more destructive than most. Please . . . Lisa . . . let me help you. You don't want to stay like this, neither dead nor living.'

He sank to his knees, watching the tears track down her cheeks. She turned her pretty face up to him and he pulled her into a hug.

'I can help you,' he said.

'Can you?' she murmured, like a little girl.

'You know I can. I will be able to help *all* the COLAs one day. Trust me. Help me find Mia and I can make everything right.'

Lisa pressed her face into his shoulder and he felt her warm breath and tears seep through his shirt. If she wasn't careful, he might be about to forgive the little wildcat and change his mind about taking her, too.

Then she kissed his cheek. And pulled away, smiling. Something in the smile sent a shard of ice though his soul.

'*Thanks*, Marcus,' she said. 'I didn't know where she was. But I do now.'

'HOW?' he bellowed, ready to tear her hair from her scalp, construct or not.

'I got it from *you* . . . well, from Olu, actually,' she said, springing to her feet. 'Olu knows . . . he just doesn't *know* he knows . . . He's still in too much shock. But it's right there in his head and right now he's hanging onto you—so it's just come straight through from him to you to me! And you didn't even notice! *Peach!*'

'And now you're going to tell ME!' growled Marcus.

'You think?' grinned Lisa, her hands on her hips. 'Sylv . . . get him out of here will you?'

He didn't see Lisa's spirit guide before she hit him on the side of his head with what felt like a breeze block. When he opened his eyes he was slumped on the thickly carpeted floor of his own home, Olu gripping his shoulder and staring at him in horror.

'You collapsed!' breathed Olu. 'I thought you were dead!'

'Take me BACK!' bawled Marcus, springing to his feet.

'I can't! Darren's raised the alarm! He started yelling as soon as you collapsed. We'll never reach Lisa again now,' said Olu.

Marcus punched the wall and then grabbed

Olu roughly by the shoulders. 'WHERE did you drop her? Where is MIA? You KNOW, don't you— you KNOW?'

Olu looked horrified and Marcus knew at once that he wasn't lying when he protested, 'If I knew, we'd have her! I would NEVER let you down, Granite. You know that! Even after the magnetite thing . . . even after I found out you were controlling me with it and not telling me . . . I still stayed. I'm still with you!'

He let the boy go and sat down, regaining his calm. 'I'm sorry, Olu. I do know.'

'Hypnotize me!' said Olu, holding up his palms. 'Get into my head and find out where she is!'

But the man only laughed and said, 'Oh, poor Olu . . . I already *have* hypnotized you. Three times now. I couldn't find it then and I won't find it now. But Lisa Hardman . . . *has.*'

'Not much good to anybody, though, eh?' muttered Olu. 'When she's in a coma.'

'True,' said Marcus, battling to keep a surge of rage under when he thought of how the girl had played him. 'Let's hope she stays that way. When we get Spook back we may well have another way to find Mia. She loves Spook. Sooner or later she's going to try to find him . . . and then we'll have her. Olu—I need you back at Fenton Lodge. Watch from the tree. Spook could be coming out any time now. I think it will be soon.'

Olu rolled his eyes. The lookout tree near the Containment block exit was uncomfortable—and very boring.

'Take supplies with you,' went on Marcus. 'If we miss Spook because you get the urge for a Mars bar I shall be *most* displeased. And make sure that scalpel stays in your hand at all times. You won't have a chance to fish it out of your pocket.'

Olu shrugged and disappeared.

*It's just a matter of time*, Marcus told himself. Chambers couldn't keep Spook in lockdown for ever without any evidence. The boy's family was wealthy and influential. As soon as they found out there would be hell to pay. He might even tip them off himself.

Sometime soon Spook would emerge into the daylight and then Olu, as long as he was fast enough with the blade, would have him . . .

# 21

The whole day might have ended just fine if it wasn't for Nell.

Mia had kept busy and was feeling much steadier as a result of all the black obsidian in her pockets—as well as the bit she'd managed to attach to some string and tie around her neck. Brigid had gone home after lunch, leaving her in the pleasant company of Niamh and Mary and assorted customers in the café and baths.

As she emptied, cleaned, and refilled the seaweed baths, she was also pondering that the Effect might actually help. She could take her foot massaging skills down to the beach tomorrow lunchtime—approach the older people and do them a service in return for—what—ten euros? If she left the obsidian behind in the cafe, the Effect would do all the rest for her. In fact, she could probably just charm the money directly out of their pockets, but that would make her a beggar . . . or a con artist . . . and she couldn't have that. No—she would heal for money. And soon she would have enough to slip away in the night from Brigid and Donal's house. Leave them a letter maybe . . . get to Dublin and start to live as anonymously as she could.

It was a good day. She had a plan—and the black obsidian against her skin was toughening her up to cope with anything.

Then Nell arrived. And for the first time in her life, said something.

Peering across a glass of pink milkshake, Nell fixed her large brown eyes on Mia, who was helping out at the till, and said, 'You're sad about your daddy.'

There had been some gentle hubbub in the café but Mia heard the child clearly. She froze, her eyes locked on Nell's.

Niamh froze too, halfway through bringing a jacket potato out of the little oven behind the counter. She stood, also staring across the counter at Nell, her mouth an O of surprise. Then the potato burnt her skin and she squeaked and dropped it on the floor. 'Did you hear that?' she demanded of Mia. 'Maria! Did you hear Nell? She spoke! She *spoke*!'

Mia ran.

She pushed the countertop up and sprinted past it and out into the buffeting sea breeze, her heart crashing in her ribcage and the blood pressure pounding in her ears as she scrambled up the steep hillside behind the café. She heard a shout from Niamh, who had come out of the building to stare after her in shock. Mia didn't look back . . . she was running in panic, but it wasn't the bathhouse she was running from. It was the memory. The memory was coming back and it was terrible. Her body had reacted with flight, to something from which she could not possibly escape. Something spilling out inside her own head.

Blindly she tore across the narrow coast road, getting hooted by a passing van as it swerved to avoid her, and ran up the steep slope on the other side—one of the foothills of a mountain range that stretched across the peninsular. She ran for half an hour, tracking up through the natural gullies formed by rainwater, splashing through cold streams, across the peak, and down the other side, well out of sight of the coast road. On the far slope she scrambled and slid further still. Low cloud enveloped her, coating her hot face in cool droplets and muffling the sound of someone crying, wailing, sobbing. It was only when she flung herself inside a pile of stones and the sound flatly echoed off the walls around her that she realized she *herself* was making that noise.

And here, inside one of the beehive stone huts that she'd seen dotted around the hills and pictured on postcards for tourists, her memory caught up. On the damp earth floor she curled into a foetal position as it arrived.

'You're sad about your daddy,' Nell had said.

Definitely psychic, then. And gentle with it. Perhaps Nell had been too kind to say, 'You killed your daddy.'

Dax met Owen and Tyrone at the airport. They'd flown into Bournemouth, choosing the quieter route in. Nobody had blinked at the false passports they'd both obtained some years ago when they'd fled from the COLA Project. Owen was officially dead and Tyrone officially away, travelling. Chambers regarded Tyrone as a friend. He had let him go and never tried to track him down, but who knew whether there was a watch on his *real* passport? He was still very much a 'person of interest' to the British government.

Owen went by the name of Gareth Walker, while Tyrone now had the title of Stephen Roberts. They didn't attract any attention as they went through customs at Malaga and at the Bournemouth end there was even less notice taken of the man with shaggy dark hair and what might have been his younger brother.

Dax waited until Owen had picked up a hire car and was pausing at the driver door, scanning the skies—then he landed on his shoulder.

Owen couldn't help but yelp—the falcon's talons bit right through his sweatshirt. 'Dax! You need a manicure!' Dax hopped off his shoulder and onto the back seat of the hired Nissan 4 x 4 where he shifted to a grinning teenage boy.

'Good flight?' asked Tyrone over the top of the front passenger seat.

'Not bad. Hungry though,' said Dax. He'd hunted twice on his way back from Spain, taking a pigeon in Southern France and a rabbit on the coast of Cherbourg.

Tyrone handed him a giant Toblerone. 'I'd forgotten how much I miss duty-free,' he said.

Owen got in and shut the door. 'OK, Dax—we're back in the UK. Are we any closer to having a plan?'

Dax smiled and ate a triangular chunk of chocolate with more happiness than he had felt in days. 'We *are* closer,' he said. 'I've had a message.' He beamed so hard the chocolate made his jaw twinge. 'While I was flying—from Lisa.'

Now Owen spun around in his seat. 'Lisa? She's OK?'

'Not exactly—not yet,' said Dax. 'But something has happened. She was deep in a coma but somebody got through to her—kind of woke up her psychic mind.'

'Who got through to her?' asked Owen.

'Your old friend Marcus Croft.'

Owen looked horrified. 'That is seriously bad news, Dax. Marcus is ruthless. He'll have ripped her subconscious into shreds to find Mia.'

'Not according to Lisa,' said Dax. 'In fact I think her exact expression was that she "punched his lights out".'

Owen shook his head, smiling. 'Of course . . . this is *Lisa* we're talking about!'

'And . . . while he was in her head,' went on Dax, pulling silver foil off another chunk of Toblerone, 'trying to make her dowse for Mia, she picked up some information from Olu—something neither Olu nor Marcus had picked up themselves. She *found out* where Olu dropped Mia.'

Owen put the key into the ignition. 'Where are we going?'

'To Luton Airport—to catch a flight to Ireland. County Kerry,' said Dax. 'I'll be flying by DaxAir— but I think you guys will have to go from the airport . . . '

Her father hadn't been well for a long time. His liver was shot years ago, according to the doctors. Edward Cooper had been an alcoholic for most of his adult life . . . except for the five years he'd been married to Ella, Mia's mother. Once Ella had died, inexplicably, of 'natural causes' and he was left alone with a three-year-old daughter, Edward started to drink again.

He kept it under control—there was no way anyone was going to take his daughter away. He was a functioning alcoholic. He'd hung onto his job, running road repair crews for the council, and

Mia was clean, fed, and healthy, and doing well in school.

But once Mia had become a COLA and was taken away to join the others, there was little incentive left for him. The COLA project offered help—financial and medical. He was given a decent house to live in, but he missed his old neighbours in the tower block. Eventually he lost his job and then he had only his occasional visits to Mia in Cumbria to stay sober for.

In the end his liver had packed up. He was hospitalized but he wouldn't let them tell his little girl. Not until it was obvious he wasn't going to be leaving the hospital in anything other than a box. Then they called for Mia.

*Would it have made a difference if we'd called her sooner?* Chambers wondered, as he scanned the transcripts of that morning's terrible session with Spook Williams. Could she have actually saved her father—healed his liver and made him whole again? What he knew of COLA talent suggested not. For all COLAs it seemed the closer you were to someone, the harder it was to help them. Mia *had* healed her father's hangovers in the past and it had taken an appalling toll on her—and ultimately changed nothing for him. The man was set on self-destruction—and too far gone.

Maybe if she had known sooner, the whole process might have been gentler. She might have been able to accept that her father was dying and this time there was nothing she could do.

As it was, the end was terrible. Horrific. Chambers never wanted to witness anything like it again. And he'd only seen it through a security camera feed.

Mia had been taken to see her father in a private hospital in North London. She'd travelled there with two M15 minders and a female police officer who was trained in counselling young people. On the way they broke it to her that Eddie Cooper wasn't going to pull through.

Mia refused to believe them. And why should she? She had saved countless lives—brought people back from the brink of death. She was a healer of astonishing power. As far as she was concerned, this was a mission. She would make her father better—probably by this time tomorrow.

This was all in the report which followed the incident in Sideward 7.

*

Inside the stone hut, Mia saw her father's gaunt face, dull and yellow against the crisp white pillow. She was back in the hospital, where her heart felt pinched and cold, as if someone had just attached a steel bulldog clip to it. 'Oh, Dad! Why didn't you tell me?'

He smiled at her and blinked wearily. When she took his thin hand it was cool and barely able to return the squeeze. 'I wanted to see you, pet,' he whispered. 'Before I go. Tell you how special you are to me. You know that, don't you?'

'You're not going anywhere!' she retorted, taking his other hand too. 'I'm going to make you better!'

One of the minders touched her shoulder. She spun around. 'Please! Leave us alone!'

They looked at each other and nodded before retreating to the other side of the door. There were glass panels in the walls to one side of the room— they could easily watch from outside.

Mia turned back to her father. 'Can't you feel it?' she said. 'I'm sending in healing. You're going to be fine!' And yet she couldn't feel the flow. She couldn't feel the tingle of the healing leaving her skin and travelling into his. It must be what Lisa called the 'Loved Ones Buffer'. It was always harder to help the ones you loved. She must make more effort.

'It's all right, pet,' said her father. He smiled and his skin creased like parchment. 'I'm ready to go now. I hope to meet your mother—say hello from you. Tell her how well you're doing . . . '

'NO!' sobbed Mia, grabbing his hands tighter, feeling the heat rise in her fingers, *forcing* the healing through. 'You're NOT going to die! You CAN'T. I won't let you!'

'Love you . . . ' sighed her father and closed his eyes.

She wouldn't believe he was dead, that was the thing, Chambers realized. She'd gone a little mad. Something in her had snapped. And of course, the hired help from MI5 didn't know much about her ability . . . certainly nothing of her *hidden* ability. All they knew was that something insane had happened.

Inside the stone hut Mia howled with horror as she remembered what happened next. In her blind rage at her futile, stupid, *weak* healing power she had somehow *broken* something inside. Something cracked and then there was a terrible smell and screaming. *She* was screaming. Her father lay still on the pillow. His hair was in flames. In seconds the bedclothes were alight too. And she was holding his cooling hands and screaming but still pulsing out more and more healing like a bee which has been ripped apart but can't stop stinging.

And so she had killed her father. She had meant to save him but instead she incinerated him right in front of the nurses and doctors and minders. They'd come charging in with fire extinguishers of course, but they were way, way too late. By the time they'd prised Mia's fingers from her father's he was just a smoking shape in a pile of ash.

# 22

'He's had a plan in progress for months,' said Chambers, once again sitting opposite the Prime Minister.

'Marcus Croft,' sighed the PM, rubbing his brow. 'Still alive, still equipped with a teleporting COLA. I'm staggered, Chambers, that they were able to get into Fenton Lodge and reach Lisa Hardman. That really is the most appalling breach of security.'

'I agree,' said Chambers. 'And it won't happen again, sir. At least they didn't take anyone.'

'Yes—at least,' said the PM drily, examining the dark patch of magnetite under the skin of his palm. All high-ranking government officials had now had magnetite inserted as a precaution.

'We have a guard at every bedside in the medical unit,' went on Chambers. 'If they come back, they'll be seized. But they won't come back. Marcus is too smart for that.'

'Was he planning to take the girl?'

'I don't think so. According to Darren Tyler, at least. They forced him to shield them with illusion while they got into the medical room. Olu Jackson cut the magnetite out of his hand and ported him upstairs. They could have done the same to Lisa, I suppose, but they didn't. They talked about rescuing Spook but my guess is that Croft was trying to find out something from Lisa . . . about Mia. Sir . . . I don't think he *has* Mia. If he had her, he would have used *her* to reach Lisa. I can't think of any other reason why he would take such a risk, coming to the lodge—he's lost Mia and he's desperate to find her.'

'So . . . Mia may be out there somewhere on her own. Is that good?' asked the PM.

'I think so,' said Chambers. 'If we can reach her before Croft does, there's still hope.'

The PM sat back in his chair. 'Chambers . . . Croft has led you a merry dance this summer, wouldn't you say? First he shows up as some kind of Samaritan figure, apparently helping to save Luke Reader on the Isle of Wight . . . then he plucks Spook Williams out from under your nose and keeps him for ten days, hypnotizing the boy so effectively that he willingly performs his own deep mind lock to stop anyone finding out where he's been. *Then* he has his tame COLA snatch Alex and Jacob Teller away, so he can use their mimicry talents to lure you into a secret meeting . . . '

Chambers gritted his teeth. There was no denying any of it. Perhaps he was about to be replaced. 'He offered to work with us, as you know,' he said. 'Maybe it's time we negotiated with him.'

'You think you could work with him?'

'No, sir. I would have to resign. You may wish that anyway,' said Chambers, making steady eye contact. 'Perhaps when we've got through this.'

'In spite of everything,' went on the PM, 'I still believe you're the best man for this job.'

'We have intelligence now,' said Chambers. 'Information from Spook Williams now that we've unlocked his mind. We know what Croft's plan *is*. He's working his way through the COLAs whom he thinks he can manipulate. Spook was an obvious choice—damaged and emotionally neglected. It seemed the Teller brothers *weren't* good material—

he's made no further attempt to get to them. I suspect he had Luke Reader in his sights for a while, but according to the psychics who got into Spook's deep mind, Mia has long been Croft's main target. And as useful as Spook would be to him, I think his plan was always to use him to get Mia. Mia cares for the boy, you see.'

'Aah,' said the PM.

'So Spook was thoroughly programmed, while he was with Croft, to manipulate Mia—to extract her from her strong friendships with Lisa Hardman, Dax Jones, and Gideon Reader and to gain her sympathy and . . . love. Then Spook, with his illusion powers, was to help create an incident which would convince her that she had no future with Cola Club. I don't think even Croft expected it to go the way it did, though.'

'Do you think Croft knew she was a pyrokinetic? Before we did?' asked the PM.

'Yes,' sighed Chambers. 'But there's another reason he wants her . . . a reason why he's gone to such an effort to set all this up, rather than just having Olu port in and grab her from the grounds one day. I've done some investigation of my own . . . on Croft's DNA.'

The PM sat up straight again. 'And . . . ?'

'You're not going to like it.'

Mia cried herself hoarse and then fell into a deep, dreamless sleep. When she woke she wished the ancient stones of the beehive hut had fallen in on her. She had killed her father. Knowing he was gone made her understand what he had been to her. It hadn't even occurred to her before, but Eddie Cooper was the bond between herself and the normal world. Without him she felt like she might just float away or dissolve. She missed that bond SO much. Her father. Her only family. Gone now. With him still in this world she might have been able to bear what else she now knew.

She knew she had killed others too.

The memories were almost back now, dancing darkly in the corners of her mind. How many? How badly had she lost control? And how much had *they* meant to her? It was a horrific train of thought and yet something in her needed to *know*. If she *was* going to step off the clifftop to make amends, she wanted first to know exactly what else she was making amends *for*.

More memory would return. She just had to

wait. And while she waited she had to keep away from people. It was obvious that people who cared about her came to pay a heavy price for it. She was friendless. She was fatherless. And that was for the best.

Outside it was dark and cold. She guessed it was mid-evening by the height of the moon. She needed her mind to work now—to start delivering those memories. It would help to get warm. She crawled from the hut and stood up on the steep hillside. The low cloud had lifted and the moon lit the pasture around her, picking out distant sheep and gleaming on the dry stone walls. Here and there were low, windswept bushes. Mia made for the nearest and began pulling twigs and sprigs off it. She returned to the hut with an armful of wood and a broken crate she'd found in a ditch. It wasn't ideal for a fire—some of it damp and green—but she had a feeling that for *her* this would not be a problem. She dropped it all on the floor, noting the hole at the top of the structure which would act as a chimney.

She built a fire as she'd been taught, years ago, by Owen Hind, their first and best teacher at Cola Club. Once it was ready—a dark pile in a shaft of moonlight—she sat back and stared at it. In seconds, at her bidding, the kindling—the drier twigs and leaves—burst into flame. Soon the crate caught too and the little hut was filled with warmth. As the smoke rose she told it to curl and then twist and then feed out in thin grey fingers, through the many chinks in the ceiling of the hut. She did not want a thick column of it seen from outside. The smoke obeyed her. It even stopped in its flow when it came within several centimetres of her face. And then it thickened and darkened across the doorway, shielding the golden light of its source so the fire would not be seen from outside. Amid all the dread and horror of the last few hours, Mia felt a raw, thin joy spiral up through her. This was *hers*. She was a fire starter. She was a healer but now . . . even more . . . a fire starter. She could control that life-giving, life-taking element. *What* a power.

Chambers was getting back into the chopper in the mid-evening when the call came through. It was everything he had been praying for since he took his leave of the Prime Minister. At last—a break.

An Irish couple had reported a missing person—a teenager called Maria, who had arrived suddenly in their lives three days ago. They had been looking after her while they worked out what to do, not wanting to possibly expose her to an abusive family before they knew the facts—or so they'd told the local Garda. And they'd only spoken up now because the girl had apparently panicked and run away again and they were too concerned to keep the secret any longer.

Within an hour of the local police report, it was all over the British intelligence network and delivered to Chambers.

'Have we enough fuel to fly out to County Kerry?' he asked the pilot.

The pilot said yes.

# 23

Spook lay slumped on the sofa in Containment. It had been hours since the attack and he ached still. But the physical assault was nothing. He felt violated in a far worse way.

After they'd forced their way into his mind he'd fought to keep them out, despite the terrible exhaustion brought on by the injection, for as long as a minute. But then the barrier had crumbled and they'd grubbed all the way through his secrets; he was powerless to stop them.

They learned about The Collector. They saw how Spook had been taken from the wreckage of the coach crash in the early summer and spirited into another world, where The Collector *had* manipulated him, true ... but then saved him; showed him how fantastic his life could be away from Cola Club. Offered him a *future*.

Sartre told him he'd been brainwashed but he knew he *belonged* with The Collector. His future lay nowhere else.

After the mind-muggers had finished with him, Chambers and his two henchmen had put him back to bed, fully clothed, to sleep off the drug which had so weakened him. He wasn't asleep, though. His eyes were closed but he was aware of everything from the snipping away of the plastic ties at his wrists and the extraction of his fingers from the solid gel to the drool which ran out of his mouth and down his chin while his head lolled, helplessly.

The henchman who'd injected him had told Chambers he would be out for the count for the rest of the day . . . but just before Spook *did* slip into unconsciousness, he heard something quite useful.

'Will he be all right when he wakes up?' Chambers had asked, touching Spook's forehead and doing a good impression of acting like he cared. 'It must have been horrific for him.'

'Can't speak for what your psychics did to him,' said the bald man. 'That's not my area. But this drug is usually fine. Some people have a delayed reaction—breathing problems—but it's very rare and there's nothing in his notes to suggest he will.'

'Well, the physical reaction is the least of our problems,' said Chambers, as they'd left the room. 'The boy's psychologically wrecked. I don't know if . . . ' And then his voice had tailed off as they closed the door.

Spook had remembered it all when he woke up and staggered out to the main room, planning his escape as he dropped onto the sofa.

Could he play the innocent victim? Agree that he *had* been brainwashed and was now horrified at what he'd done? Would they believe it? He didn't think so. His whole inner psyche had been raked over by those disgusting psychics and they must have worked out that his loyalty lay with The Collector.

So . . . how would he ever get out of this place? The Collector had told him he would be rescued— but gave him no details of how. Just as well, he guessed, after what had happened in his head today.

But Spook knew enough about Olu's talents to understand he must get outside. The teleporter couldn't get into the lodge or its underground complex because he hadn't seen it—or any pictures of it. But he'd seen all the outside areas. Any rescue would happen in the open air. But how to get there . . . ?

His mind went back to that conversation between the bald thug and Chambers. What would they *do* if he went into some kind of shock or seizure— breathing problems? Would they rush him up to the medical wing? Spook thought so . . .

Of course, they might just bring the doctor down *here* . . . but if he was convincing enough they might not feel they had time.

Spook needed to create his best ever illusion to pull this off. It had to marry with an Oscar- worthy acting performance. He was already sweaty and clammy. That would help. Spook peered, through half closed lids, at the security camera in the top corner of the room. Would they be watching?

Certainly they would. Spook suddenly arched his back and made a gargling, gasping noise. He sent his limbs into violent trembles. With the ebbing effects of the drug still in his system, it was easy to do. Just a *little* panic juice . . . and then he pulled his focus in tight and sent an illusion across every inch of his body. Inside, he was just fine. But from the outside his face had swollen . . . his eyes were just pale slits in his face, his lips were blue.

It took them a minute to get in there. The bald man was bending over him along with two others he didn't recognize. 'What is it?' said one of them. 'Is it a stunt?'

They touched his skin and felt the clamminess and the sweat and the intense shaking which crashed through his muscles like a bodily earthquake.

'Feels pretty real,' said one of them. 'I don't think he'd have the strength to throw an illusion just yet.'

*Ha!* thought Spook. *You really don't know about COLA strength, do you, friend?*

A minute later they had him on a stretcher. 'Get him up to medical *now*,' said the henchman.

'Shouldn't we run this past Chambers?' asked another.

'He's with the Prime Minister,' came the reply. 'Can't be reached. I'm calling this—get him to medical! And call the principal. She'll want to get the healers in too.'

Spook was raced up the stairwell and out into the evening light. In the midst of his physical and illusory performance he still thought to lay his right hand out, palm up, as soon as he felt the fresh air on his face.

Four seconds later his hand was sliced open and the lozenge of magnetite flipped out. Even as the men around him yelled out in shock, Spook felt himself evaporate from their world.

# 24

He fell onto a carpeted floor, his head spinning and his left palm gushing blood. Olu hadn't had time for precise surgery. It was a slash and grab. The wound was deep.

The Collector leaned over him and grabbed his shoulders. 'Spook! Welcome back!'

Spook got up on one elbow and felt relief course through him. The Collector's grasp sent in a calmness, steadying his breathing and banishing the nausea.

'Here,' said Olu. There was the click and hiss of a can being opened. 'Have some of this; it'll help with the shock. First port is always a bit throwy-uppy.'

'It's not my first port, though, is it?' said Spook, trying hard to regain some dignity. He hated to be sprawling on the floor while Olu stood around looking like he did this every day. 'You've ported me before, haven't you?' He took the Coke from Olu and sipped at it.

'Doesn't miss a trick, this one!' said Olu, chirpily. 'But the other times you were unconscious, so they don't count.'

'Here—let me sort this out,' said The Collector, deftly applying first cotton wool to his lacerated hand and then a bandage. A first aid kit lay on the table. 'Good job, Olu,' he said, drily. 'Glad you missed the artery.'

'Look—*you* try doing it in three seconds flat!' protested Olu, leaning against the pine-clad wall of the lofty hexagonal room. 'That's all I had before his bodyguards would've grabbed us.'

'He did well,' admitted Spook, sitting up fully now and nodding at Olu. 'Thanks for getting me out of there.'

'You need rest,' observed The Collector.

'No I don't,' said Spook. 'I've been "resting" all day. I've had enough of it. Where's Mia? I want to see her.'

'Ah,' said The Collector. 'Of course. You don't know.'

175

'What?' Instantly Spook was alert. 'What's happened to her?'

'We're not sure,' said The Collector. 'I'm afraid your little stunt on Monday worked slightly too well. It definitely did what we hoped for—alienated Mia completely from her old life—but there was a hiccup. When Olu took her she was . . . out of control.'

Spook looked more closely at Olu and noted, with a thud of shock, the burn scars down one side of his face and across the backs of his hands.

'And so I'm afraid he dropped her.'

'He *what?*' Spook shot to his feet and then had to grab the window sill to stay upright.

Olu glowered at him. 'I was *on fire!*' he growled. 'I couldn't *help* it.'

'Where?' demanded Spook, his heart throbbing hard in his chest. He felt a fresh heat in the cotton wool on his hand as blood surged out of it.

'Olu—could you please ask Mrs Rabley to make us some tea and sandwiches?' Olu stared angrily at The Collector, clearly aware that he was being got rid of. 'And—walk in please . . . let's not give her a heart attack.'

Olu stalked out of the room. The Collector steered Spook to seats at the table and sat with him. 'This is our problem,' he said. 'Olu can't remember. Despite my best efforts he was in shock and in a great deal of pain for two days. I have tried to retrieve this memory from him but to no avail.'

'So—what now? How are we going to find her?' Spook heard his voice getting high and panicky.

'I *did* attempt to get Lisa Hardman to assist,' said The Collector.

'Hardman? I thought she was dead!' said Spook.

'In a coma . . . not dead,' said The Collector. 'I managed to get to her, with Olu's help, and visit her deep subconscious. It was . . . unsuccessful. Except . . . '

'Go on,' said Spook, staring into the man's icy blue eyes.

'What it did reveal is that Olu *does* know where he dropped Mia . . . Lisa found that information in him when I couldn't, because Olu was in physical contact with me while I was visiting her feisty little psyche. It was . . . galling, I admit, that *she* got to it when I couldn't. But at least I know it *is* in his head. It's just a question of how we retrieve it. And now you're back with me, I think I have found the way.

We need to retread the path of memory his shock has blocked out.'

'How do we do that?' asked Spook.

'*You* do it, Spook. Are you up to an illusion of the first order?'

'Of course,' said Spook, wondering why The Collector was reaching into the first aid kit for scissors.

'Good,' said the man. 'I think I can help a little too.' He snipped off several chunks of his thick white hair and dropped them into a shallow glass bowl. Then he pulled a silver lighter out of his pocket and put a flame to the hair. At once a pungent smell filled the room.

The Collector grimaced. 'Most unpleasant . . . but evocative,' he said. 'Here comes Olu now, Spook. I think you know what to do.'

Spook nodded, feeling slightly sick again. He had never done anything quite as horrific as this.

Olu strolled back in, sniffing at the air with a look of fearful recognition.

And Spook set him on fire.

# 25

*Spook loves me.* Mia turned over, the hot embers sending red light across her face and the smoke still obediently locking out the dawn light. *He knows what I am and he still accepts me.*

This is what he had told her when they brought her back from the hospital where her dead father lay. Mia opened her mind to the memory and let it slide in.

She had been hysterical at the hospital. They'd had to sedate her. As soon as she came around in a bed in the Fenton Lodge medical unit she had asked for Spook.

'You want to see *Spook*?' Janey had queried, her brow creased. 'Don't you mean Lisa?'

'Spook,' she had repeated. 'Not Lisa.'

'She's been desperate to see you,' went on the doctor. 'And Dax and Gideon too. They've been

179

so worried about you. We all have. You've been through a terrible time.'

'Will you ask Spook to come or do I have to go and find him myself?' she had said.

At this Janey had straightened up. 'Of course. I'll send for him.'

Spook had arrived looking pale and stricken, the late afternoon sun sending a halo around the back of his dark red hair as he sat beside the bed and bent his head low towards hers. He took her hand. 'I heard what happened,' he whispered. 'Mia, I'm so sorry.' His lips brushed her fingers. 'But you'll never be alone. I will always be here for you. Whatever you do.'

She stared at him. Did he know? They'd told her it wasn't her fault. It was some awful freak accident. So terrible. But her father hadn't suffered. He was gone before the fire. The doctors all agreed he had not suffered at all . . .

But Spook seemed to see inside her. He *knew* she'd done it. That it *was* her fault. Her eyes filled with tears and he stroked her hair.

'Whatever they say to you, remember this,' he murmured. 'You are exceptional. You cannot be bound by the normal laws of this planet. You are above them. Like a goddess.'

'I don't want to be,' she'd whimpered. 'I just want it all to go away. It hurts so much. Make it go away, Spook, please.'

'Watch,' said Spook. He cupped his hands and a drift of deep violet smoke began to pour into them, from her ribcage, just where her wrecked heart lay. It poured in twisted, turbulent lines and then settled in a cloud around his long fingers, tailing off to a thin vapour at her heart. 'This is the pain,' he said. And then a box appeared on the bed. A square, cardboard box with a purple ribbon tied around it. As she stared in amazement, the ribbon undid itself, the lid of the box lifted, and the smoke slid into it. When it was fully inside, the box lid closed and the ribbon tied itself.

'We know where this pain is,' said Spook. 'It's here—in the box. You can find it if you need to . . . but you won't need to. You've had enough. Here it goes . . . ' And he cast it away over his shoulder. It vanished mid-trajectory.

And then he'd kissed her and she couldn't think about the box any more. After he'd left, promising to be back very soon, a kind of numbness lay where the pain had been. 'You are above them,' he'd said.

'Like a goddess.'

When Lisa and Dax and Gideon came to see her she was able to smile at them. And when they spoke to her she didn't absorb a word they said.

'She's special,' said Brigid, her face pale and taut with control as she made tea for the man from the British government.

He'd arrived the night before, according to Garda Finn Malone, but had been held off from visiting them until dawn while a search of the coast and mountains was organized from a control centre in Tralee. Barely dawn! It was 5 a.m. when the knocking started. Now, at 5.15, she was in her nightie and bathrobe, making tea, while Donal glowered mistrustfully at the government man and Malone who was lounging on the couch like he owned it.

'We know,' said Chambers. 'That's why we need to find her—quickly. She's in danger. I mean . . . in more danger than most. Tell me how you found her.'

'Donal found her on the beach,' said Brigid, setting the mugs on the table next to the photo of Maria—no, *Mia*—the Englishman had brought.

'Lying there for all the world as if dead. She'd . . .' she paused, looking uncomfortable, 'no clothes on. And some burns on her skin. We brought her in and gave her a seaweed bath and some food and . . . rest.'

'Did she tell you anything about herself?' Chambers addressed this to Donal directly.

'No,' he said, staring at his hands. 'Just her name—Maria.'

'Are you sure?' asked Chambers. He waited for Donal to look up at him before continuing: 'Because it looks to me as if she *did* tell you something and you're just not wanting to tell me.'

Donal stood up and glared at the English interloper. 'Are you calling me a liar? Is this how it goes?' There was no way he was going to reveal what she'd said to him in the caves . . . *I will hurt you. I won't mean to. But that doesn't mean it won't happen.* It was burnt into his memory, but he'd never even told Brigid *that*.

Chambers accepted his mug of tea from Brigid with a smile and sipped it. 'Mr O'Malley—I'm very, very grateful to you for helping Mia. And for agreeing to help me find her. A nasty shock for you both, some English suit showing up on your doorstep at this ungodly hour. And you still made me tea. It's clear you are decent, caring people and I completely understand your reasons for keeping Mia safe with you for a few days while you tried to find out more about her situation. She is, as you say, very special. Very easy to love.'

Donal and Brigid exchanged a glance which confirmed what Chambers already knew—that Mia had not lost the Effect. He also knew she'd done more than just give them the warm fuzzies. On the way through the mountains in Garda Malone's jeep, he'd picked that up fast. 'Donal was beside himself when he came in to report to me,' the officer had said. 'I've never seen him like it—jumping all over the show about this Maria girl, like she was his own daughter. And him with terrible arthritis too— you'd never have known it to look at him yesterday. He *ran* into the station, I tell you!' That was when Chambers had known for sure that this 'Maria' was Mia.

Brigid sat down opposite Chambers. 'She had amnesia . . . at least, that's what she told us. And— with the burns and all that—we wanted to wait until she was ready to tell us. She was getting better. She did some work with me up at my bathhouse.

I wanted to keep her close, you understand—keep her busy and talking to my ladies there—see whether it helped.'

'And did it?' asked Chambers.

'It seemed to. She was brighter and steadier. And she went back again yesterday and then . . . something happened. Our Nell spoke up.'

'Our Nell?' echoed Chambers.

'Yes—a little girl who comes into the bathhouse café from time to time. One of my staff, Niamh, is a friend of her mother and sometimes we babysit her for a while. She's a lovely little thing. Nearly five.'

'And what did Nell say?'

'Well it's not so much *what* she said,' explained Brigid. 'I'm not sure what she *did* say, exactly. It's that she said *anything*. You see, Nell doesn't speak. She hasn't spoken at all since she was born! But yesterday . . . she did. And it was then that Maria—I mean, Mia—ran off. Like something possessed, Niamh said. Niamh went after her—but Mary had to hold the fort and watch Nell. Niamh lost her . . . she thinks she reached the road and maybe got a lift from a passing car. She could be anywhere. Donal got up some friends to search the mountains but they couldn't find her and then the cloud came

185

down and it was too dangerous anyway . . . and . . .
I just think . . . ' Brigid swallowed and her eyes
glittered in the lamplight, ' . . . I think our time
was up. Maria had to move on. We'd had all we
were due.'

Chambers eyed her with interest. 'What *had*
you had?'

Brigid lifted her chin. 'I don't expect you to
understand,' she said.

'Try me,' he answered.

'She was a blessing. Something about her . . .
changed things. Donal got better. Nell started to
speak. Mary says her eczema has gone—for the first
time in twelve years! Even my neighbour in the gift
shop told me . . . Maria *healed her feet*! She *did*. Like
some kind of . . . ' she dropped her eyes to the
table and murmured, ' . . . angel.'

She glanced up defensively, clearly expecting
scorn, but Chambers only nodded and said, 'So . . .
nothing *bad* happened. Only the good stuff, yes?'

'Nothing but good,' said Donal. 'She's a good
girl. Better than good. Find her and keep her safe.'

Chambers stood up and shook his hand, noting
the firm grip and the supple knuckles and feeling
a twinge, in himself, of something like pride and

misery entwined. 'We will find her,' he said. 'And keep her safe.'

'Will you take her back to her family?' asked Brigid.

'She has no family,' said Chambers. 'But she has friends who love her. Trust me—I'll do the very best I can for her.' He held out his hand to Brigid.

She took it, looking at him intently. 'I believe you will, Mr Chambers.'

Chambers didn't hold her gaze for long.

# 26

'She was here,' said Dax. 'I can smell it.'

Owen crouched by the dead fire in the middle of the beehive hut and shone his torch around the small structure.

'How long ago?'

Dax inhaled and closed his eyes. 'Less than an hour.'

'Handy, that nose of yours,' said Owen. 'Can you follow her scent outside?'

Dax looked doubtful. 'Maybe—but it's windy and wet. I don't know how reliable it'll be. I should fly around the area a bit more and try to spot her.'

Owen sat down and motioned the boy to do the same. 'You've flown thousands of miles; you're knackered.'

Dax felt a tug towards the air. 'Mia's in danger—I know it. I can't wait.'

They had split up, with Tyrone heading along the high ridge to the north while Dax and Owen stayed near the coast. Lisa's messages were not too clear—after all, she *was* still in a coma. Inside Dax's falcon mind, she had been sometimes incoherent and sometimes sharp and loud—like someone talking in their sleep. But she had sent them to this small coastal community—Ballytreen—speaking of mountains and sea. She hadn't said which side they needed to get to.

'Dax—you should remember—Mia may not be . . . ' began Owen.

'In her right mind?' said Dax.

'She's been through something terrible,' said Owen. 'We don't know what it's done to her. If you see her, come back to me. Please don't fly straight to her.'

'Do you think she's going to blast me out of the sky on a jet of flame?' Dax stared at Owen.

'Isn't that pretty much what she did the last time you saw her?' asked Owen, with a rueful smile.

'No!' Dax felt himself flush with anger. 'Not— not deliberately! She was confused—someone messed her up. She wasn't . . . '

'In her right mind?' Owen sighed. 'You see my point.'

'I do,' admitted Dax. 'But you don't understand mine. You weren't there.' He could wait no longer. He shifted and flew away.

Mia took a long drink from a mountain spring which dripped through rocks. Remembering Spook had made her feel peculiar—swimmy-headed. It was as if the returning memories were only half her own . . . and half scripted by someone else. Mia leaned into a cleave of dark, moss-covered rock, closed her eyes and returned to Fenton Lodge. Her very last day there . . .

She had been back on her feet the day after she'd killed her father, although nobody expected her to attend lessons. She was checked over by Janey and then again, in Development, by Mrs Sartre, who told her—for the fifth or sixth time—that her father's death was not her fault. But Mia didn't have to be a mind reader to see that they had all changed. For the first time, they *knew*. She was not what she had seemed. She was no longer harmless.

Of course, Dax, Lisa, and Gideon had known

for two years or more that she was a pyrokinetic—possibly even before she had known herself. That she was a killer, they also knew. She had killed Catherine—Gideon and Luke's triplet sister—the rogue COLA who would have murdered all the others. There really had been no choice when Mia sent Catherine to her death in a ball of flame high above the North Sea. But Dax had *seen* her do it. He knew she had done it to save his life . . . to save them all . . . but had he seen that most terrifying facet of his friend? That merciless streak. Had he seen Mia smile?

'You're not like them,' Spook had told her, more than once. 'They don't know what's on the other side of you. I don't think they can handle it, do you?'

'They might know,' she had said. 'They might understand . . . '

'Trust me—it's all very black and white for them,' Spook had told her. 'Good or bad—nothing in between.'

At lunchtime they came looking for her—Dax, Gideon, and Lisa. They headed straight for the tree house, a little way into the woods, where they *knew* she'd be. Well, of course—Lisa would have dowsed for her. As she heard them approaching, before they were fully in sight, Mia climbed down and moved stealthily towards the approaching party, hiding behind a tree before they could see her. Lisa, when she came into view, was edgy, glancing around. Mia heard Lisa say, 'I don't know what to think . . . I can't trust my own instincts any more.'

*No,* thought Mia. *You probably shouldn't. Your best friend's a killer.* She took a deep breath and thought of the box where Spook had hidden her grief. Maybe she could get him to open another one and put all her softness about her friends into it too . . . that way she didn't need to fear their scorn or their pity. *'First she kills Gideon's sister,'* she heard Dax say, *'and now it's her own dad. Who's going to be next?'* This was in her mind . . . and yet it seemed as real as the conversation reaching her ears.

They were almost at the tree house now. Lisa rubbed her left shoulder and shivered. 'This is freaking me out,' she told Dax and Gideon.

'We're all spooked,' said Gideon. 'Speaking of which, did you see Spook creeping about in the corridor outside the medical room? All over Mia like a rash . . . I can't believe they let *him* see her when they didn't let us.'

'I don't like it,' said Lisa, pausing, with a shudder. She lowered her voice, glancing in the direction of the tree house. 'He's been trying to slime his way into her life for years . . . but the last few weeks, I don't know. It looks like he's succeeded. She doesn't tell me things any more . . . not like she used to. I think she talks to *him*.'

'Is she right?' came a soft voice, just behind her, and she felt Spook slide his hands around her waist. 'You don't have to deal with them now,' he whispered. 'They just can't wait to pick over all the gory details of what happened, can they? Vultures. You don't have to feed them.'

'I don't want to,' she whispered back, although sorrow seemed to drip from her heart, like lifeblood. 'It's too painful.'

'Then don't,' said Spook. 'If you can't trust people, you have to cut them out of your life.' He took her hand and led her quietly away to the edge of the wood. Mia wondered if Dax would pick up her scent and follow, but he didn't, walking on, instead, with his two best friends.

'You need to be brave, Mia,' said Spook, as they reached the edge of the woods. 'And I know you can be.' He sat her down on a stone bench which was covered with a wooden arch festooned in rambling roses. Here, in this pretty setting, just a short walk from the lodge, with the late summer birds chirping gently, he took out a blade. It was a scalpel-sharp thing which looked like it might have come from the art store at the lodge. 'We have to get rid of this too . . . ' He turned over her palm and pressed against the faint grey lozenge-shaped shadow. 'Because we can't trust it.'

Mia felt her heartbeat speed up but she knew pain was fleeting—nothing but a means to an end. She closed her eyes and nodded. *What she didn't trust, she must cut out. He was right. Maybe it was the magnetite that had messed up her healing power . . .* The sharp cut made her gasp but she didn't cry out. Spook excavated the wound and flicked the magnetite out quickly, then pressed a white cotton handkerchief to the blood. He had come prepared, she noted.

'Are you all right?' he asked, putting his arm around her shoulders and holding her tight.

She nodded, not trusting herself to speak yet. She didn't want to let a whimper escape her lips.

'Can you heal yourself?' he asked. 'Have you learned to do that yet?'

'No,' she managed.

'Doesn't matter,' he said and all at once she sensed great excitement in him. She could feel his heart beating fast through her shoulder and realized he was scanning the grounds agitatedly. 'Soon you'll feel much better,' he added.

'What do you mean?' She pulled away from him, staring into his eyes for the first time.

'I'm getting you out of here,' he said, a rather sickly grin winding across his face. His pupils seemed to contract as he stared around, making his eyes look like amber marbles.

'What? How?' She stood up, but he held fast to her other hand.

'It's OK, Mia!' he said. 'You'll be safe—you'll be much happier. And you can't stay here. Chambers doesn't have enough evidence to lock you up underground yet . . . but he will. Sooner or later Dax or Lisa or Gideon will tell him what they know about you. They'll confirm that you're a pyrokinetic . . . and they'll tell you they're doing it for *your* sake. And then you'll be in lockdown.'

'But . . . but they're my friends,' she'd said, wanting to erase what she'd said before—about not trusting them. Wanting to rewind it all and change it. She *needed* her friends. With her father gone, they were all she had left now!

'*I* am your friend,' said Spook, standing up and pulling her close. 'The only one you can trust. You can tell me anything! Can you tell *them*?'

'I—I don't know,' she said, feeling buffeted by panic and despair and confusion. She had *heard* Lisa say it . . . that she couldn't trust her own instincts . . . that she was freaked out. Lisa had changed. Could Mia really trust her any more?

'Lisa's jealous of you,' said Spook, as if he were reading her mind. 'She hates it that people notice you more than her. You know she can't stand not being the centre of attention.'

'She's not . . . She isn't . . . ' Mia protested but she heard the doubt in her own voice.

'And Gideon's a fool—he can't possibly understand you.'

Mia tried to draw air in through her lungs and found it thick and clammy. She was shaking . . . with what? Fear? Anger? Excitement? She couldn't pick the emotions apart.

'And Dax Jones . . . the Prime Minister wrote him a letter of thanks after that little jaunt with Lisa in London, did you know? He's a good government boy. Playing it straight for five gold stars and a sticker! He really *won't* understand you—ever.'

Mia struggled to breathe. Panic surged up and down her body and she felt sweat prickle across her back.

'I bet they're all sitting there in the tree house trying to work out who's going to go to Chambers first,' went on Spook. 'Which one of them gives him the full story on lovely Mia—healer and fire starter.'

'They wouldn't!' cried out Mia. Even though she was feeling feverishly hot, her teeth were chattering.

Spook grabbed her and spun her around to face him. 'They *would*, Mia! They would! This is what I've been trying to tell you—but they've really had you convinced, for so long now, that they're completely on your side. Why are they still over there, eh, if they haven't found you? Why isn't Lisa dowsing for you again and coming to find you? Because now they want to talk *about* you—not *to* you!'

'But . . . ' Mia felt the atmosphere around her grow thin and hot. 'Spook . . . I can't . . . I can't . . .' Emotional pain, like a twisting knife in her ribs, shot through her as she took in his words. Her heart seemed to be thundering in her throat and the world was hazy . . .

. . . and then there was a bright flash. From far away she heard Spook cry out, 'Oh my God! Oh my God—Mia! What have you done?'

Over in the wood there was a funnel of red-gold flame hurling itself into the sky. Then a white hot explosion sent cracked branches and planks of wood in all directions.

'The tree house! You've torched the tree house!' yelled Spook, raking his hands through his hair in horror. 'Oh my God!'

Mia could not believe what she was seeing. She fell to her hands and knees, trying to suck in air. Had she just . . . ? Had she . . . ? NO! It wasn't possible! She couldn't have killed her friends!

'Oh my God . . . it's like with your dad!' she heard Spook gasp. 'They'll all be dead! Oh Mia . . . oh, my poor Mia. The soldiers are coming! They'll be coming for you now!'

And they *were* coming. They must have been prepared for what destruction she might bring about, because suddenly three people were running from the woods. At first it seemed to be Lisa, Dax, and Gideon, yelling her name, but when she looked again it was just men. Men in black combat outfits with helmets and guns. They were bellowing, 'GET DOWN, GET DOWN, GET DOWN!'

'You CAN'T TAKE HER!' screamed Spook, dragging her up to her feet and pinning her against his chest with both arms. 'You WILL NOT lock her away! I won't LET YOU!'

He turned her face up to his with one hand. 'MIA! You've got to stop them getting to you! They'll get you! And me! Set the ground on fire in front of them! Do it NOW!' And he swung her around, directing her at the incoming military men. 'DO IT!' he hissed.

Still she quailed. She didn't want to, in spite of the build-up of heat she could feel in her fingers and her solar plexus. Then she saw a small black helicopter rise up behind the men. She heard the communications. *TAKE HER OUT! TAKE THEM BOTH OUT! WE HAVE NO CHOICE!*

'Now, Mia! Do it! Do it NOW!' screamed Spook.

Flame erupted across the grass—a barrier of white and yellow heat, shooting up into the sky and blocking off the approaching men. She saw them flung back, arms and legs flailing, before the wall of fire was too thick and high to see through. And then it tore furiously across the Fenton Lodge gardens towards the house. Rose bushes popped and hissed in the flower beds and a finger of flame shot up into the sky and reached the helicopter. Perhaps some part of her had meant only to scare the pilot away, but there was no denying the punch of sharp satisfaction she felt when the chopper exploded.

Spook still held her, his heart beating so fast through her back she began to imagine they had fused into one being and were sharing the same surging blood supply.

'Hang on! Hang on, Mia!' he called. 'Take control now . . . please . . . keep it steady! My friend is coming to help. We're getting you out of here!'

And that's when the skinny black kid suddenly appeared in front of them from nowhere. Mia screamed—an unearthly, banshee-like sound. She simply could not take any more shocks.

She heard the boy shout something to Spook and Spook shout back and then the boy grabbed her—and the whole world went crushingly silent. And in that moment the biggest burst of fury she had ever felt in her life erupted from her. She felt flames engulf her—and heard the boy scream.

Then she was falling.

# 27

How The Collector made it up with Olu was beyond Spook. He had instructed him to set fire to the boy—and although he and Spook knew it wasn't for real, for Olu there were at least thirty seconds of unspeakable horror as he was 'burnt alive'. The authentic smell of singed hair was a particularly brilliant and brutal touch, thought Spook. He knew no sense could trigger buried memory faster than smell.

Olu's screams had chilled him, even as he engulfed the boy in flames, and he'd felt sick when he noticed Olu's jeans suddenly darken. The boy, in his terrible, edge-of-death panic, had wet himself. Spook suspected he had just made an enemy for life.

But it worked. Just as Olu lost bladder control,

The Collector stepped across and grasped his arms. 'WHERE ARE YOU? WHERE HAVE YOU DROPPED HER?' he yelled.

'HELP ME!' screamed Olu.

'WHERE HAVE YOU DROPPED HER?' yelled The Collector.

'IRELAND!' shrieked Olu. 'WEST COAST! Mountains and sea!' He subsided into heaving, hitching sobs and collapsed against The Collector, who soothed him while Spook snuffed out the illusion.

'Well done, Olu, well done,' said The Collector. 'And you can take us there, can you?'

Olu made a muffled noise into The Collector's shoulder. He *could* take them.

'Good boy. Now, shhhhhh. Let me make it better.'

Spook saw him rock Olu slowly from side to side and then push the boy away at arm's length, still rocking him with his hands. 'See me,' he said, and fixed those powerful eyes on Olu's as he swayed him from side to side. 'Know me. Remember we are strong. We are bonded. Family. Together we can do anything.'

Even from the other side of the room, Spook

felt the impact of the hypnosis. He realized he had been subject to this himself, possibly many times.

Soon, Olu was sitting at the table, drinking from the Coke can that Spook had only partly drained a short while ago. He steadied quickly—and then glanced across at Spook.

Spook got in first. 'Olu—I'm sorry I had to do that,' he said.

Olu just waved a contemptuous hand at him. 'It's not the worst thing anyone's done to me, Ginger,' he said.

Spook bit back a sharp retort. *Nobody* got away with calling him Ginger—or any other nickname. Not even Darren. But, in the circumstances, he'd let it go *this time.*

Olu vanished a second later.

'Will he be all right?' Spook asked.

The Collector raised an eyebrow at him. 'He'll find Mia for us . . . that's the main thing.'

'I know it is . . . but,' Spook shrugged, 'well, I guess we'll be working together a lot in future. It's not a great start, is it?'

'He'll get over it,' said The Collector. 'Like he said . . . he's suffered worse.'

Olu was back two minutes later, wearing fresh

jeans, a T-shirt, expensive trainers, and a denim jacket. He looked absolutely composed.

The Collector had pulled on a waxed cotton jacket and a soft suede trilby hat. He checked over Spook's attire—black jeans over charcoal-coloured Italian leather boots, and a fine turquoise wool jersey—and seemed to approve. 'A little well dressed to be trudging the west coast of Ireland . . . but you'll do,' he said. 'Let's go.'

'Is *he* coming too?' asked Olu, staring at Spook.

'He is,' said The Collector. 'We'll need him to look after Mia and be sure she comes to us willingly.'

'Fine,' said Olu. 'But if he pulls any more stunts with me I'll drop him in the Arctic wastes.' He grabbed their wrists and ported them all away.

As the sun filtered through the low cloud, Mia's head cleared. She sat up straight, her eyes fully open, and examined the small fire in the palm of her hand. It crackled and hissed like any fire in a grate and she could feel the heat rising from it— and yet her palm remained intact and undamaged, with just a tingling sensation beneath the tiny pyre.

This was the first time she had calmly observed her power at close quarters. It *was* amazing. And, unlike the healing, which always came at a cost, even if only temporarily, the fire did not hurt her. She made the golden flames twist into braids and coils and sent the smoke into elaborate curls, swirling through the cool air like eels in the sea. It felt *good*.

So . . . now she knew what she was. And what she had done. She had killed her father, her three best friends, possibly some soldiers, and definitely a helicopter pilot . . . maybe crew too. She was some kind of terrible force of nature . . . able to destroy lives or save them—kill or cure. She remembered what Spook had once said to her. 'You are a goddess!' Could it be true? And did that mean she was immortal, too? She had never *felt* immortal . . . but when you looked at the evidence . . .

She had been dropped into the sea from some great height. And yet she was still alive when Donal found her. Pathetic and naked . . . but still alive.

'I really have had enough of being pathetic,' she said, aloud.

The pain was still in her though—guilt at what she had done. The shock of her returning memory had left her quite numb, but she knew it wouldn't last. She and Lisa and Dax and Gideon . . . they had been through so much together. They'd saved each other's lives. She had loved them and, in spite of what had happened at the end, she knew they had loved her too. But wasn't that what always happened to mortals who loved the gods? They got burnt . . .

'Clifftop time!' said Mia, snapping the fire shut in her hand. It made sense. If she *was* immortal she would survive. If she wasn't . . . well, the full horror of her guilt would soon come to eat her up, so she might as well depart this life anyway. Maybe find her father and her mother in the afterlife. Perhaps they would forgive her. Family did that. Family had to forgive you. Didn't they?

She would get back to the sea—have a long look at the water from the clifftop. Find the right spot and then . . . if there was a heaven, and her parents—and Dax and Lisa and Gideon—were there, she could ask for forgiveness.

Tyrone took in the view of the sea from high on the mountain. It was breathtakingly beautiful. The low cloud was steadily clearing and warm shafts of early morning sun gleamed on the distant grey-blue water. Behind him, in the valley, he could see three search parties, spread far out over several miles, obviously looking for Mia. Now that the dawn had broken and the cloud had lifted he expected choppers soon, too.

Part of him hoped Chambers and his crew had already found her. If Dax and Owen got to her first it would be, at the very best, dangerous and complicated. At worst, fatal. He cared about Mia, of course, but he cared about Owen and Dax more.

The slopes of the lower peaks were grooved with many mountain streams. The water had carved deep gullies here and there and it was in one of these that Ty suddenly saw a bright golden blaze of light. He stood up, his pulse quickening, and brought his binoculars to his eyes. Whoever was making the fire was too distant for his lenses to pick out, but he could see that the flame was travelling . . . not licking along the ground or twisting through the air but moving slowly up the slope with a slight bounce, as if it were being carried.

Ty went for his radio and just at this point, Dax landed on his shoulder with a thud and a screech right in his ear. A second later the boy was standing beside him. 'Is it her?' he panted.

'I can't be sure,' said Tyrone. 'Get down there

and fly over. Come back and tell me right away!'

Dax shifted and flew down the valley. His instinct was to plummet towards the fiery glow—but memory of how he'd been knocked out of the sky by Mia's power last time held him in check. Instead, he coasted around and kept his sharp falcon eyes on the golden light. In seconds he was flipping over and shooting back to Tyrone. 'It's her!' he puffed, the second he shifted. Then he was back in bird form and flying for Owen, who was toiling along an overgrown gulley to the south.

'She's up on that slope,' he gasped, pointing to the west, as soon as he'd found Owen. 'Heading back towards the coast.'

'I know—Tyrone's just radioed it through,' said Owen. 'We're both heading after her. Dax, stay with me now. It's too dangerous for you to—'

But Owen's words were left floating on the breeze. The boy was already gone.

Chambers was in exactly the right place, on the coast road that wound along the foot of the mountains. Mia had been seen. The patrols were heading for her fast but they were on foot; the mountainous slopes were too steep for military vehicles, and in any case, he had not wanted that level of aggression, given Mia's unpredictability. If she had torched her own friends, even mistakenly, he shuddered to think what she might do to his men. They had fireproof gear on, but from what he'd seen at Fenton Lodge, he didn't think it would help much.

'Follow covertly,' he'd told Jem, his man on point in the closest team. 'But catch up as fast as you can.'

He waited in the Garda's jeep, watching the closest peak. At any moment he should see the small, dark figure of Mia crest it. The radio crackled an acknowledgement and he gave thanks for short-wave communication devices. The mobile phone coverage around here was diabolical. He plucked his Samsung out and held it aloft, vainly seeking a single bar.

'You'll be lucky, so,' observed Malone, in the driver's seat. 'Even the car phone is as much good as a paper cup and string around here! But the radio is good.'

As if to confirm his words there was another crackle and Malone snatched up the radio handset, responding with a professional vigour which

Chambers was certain was for his benefit, before passing it over to his passenger. It was news from England. Bad news. Spook Williams was gone. Snatched from a stretcher on the way to medical and teleported away. Chambers fought the urge to scream abuse at the unlucky messenger. How could they have been so *stupid*?

Instead he clamped down on his emotions and told them he would deal with it on his return. 'Take no action,' he commanded. 'Tell nobody.' At least no other COLA had witnessed it this time. It was a pitiful shred of consolation. Dear God—the Jackson boy had even known to slice the magnetite out of Spook's palm!

Malone sat bolt upright in his seat. 'Look!'

Chambers looked. And there she was . . . just beginning to climb down towards the sea.

'Keep still,' said Chambers. 'Do nothing. Say nothing.'

Malone looked disappointed. Chambers ignored him. Clearly the fool would be chasing her back over the mountain now if he had his way. Or possibly cooking in his uniform. Chambers had made him switch off the engine and lights and leave the car as if parked. At this angle to the edge of the road, the blue and yellow squares along the vehicle's flank were masked by low shrubs and the 'GARDA' lettering across the bonnet wasn't too obvious. He estimated Mia would be at least two thirds down the slope before she saw it—giving him the advantage if he had to give chase.

But he didn't want to give chase. He wanted to follow carefully; wanted the chance to talk to her, one on one, to bring her in quietly. With nobody else around, it might just be achievable. He felt a deep ache for what would follow. *Ah, Mia,* he thought. *How I wish I'd known.*


'I'm going out,' said Donal, springing up suddenly; something he could not have done a week before.

He and Brigid had not gone back to bed. They had sat at the table, drinking tea and talking, trying to make sense of the past few days.

'I'm coming too,' said Brigid. 'Let's take a walk together, along the beach. I can't remember the last time we did that.'

They dressed warmly and quickly. Neither of them could explain the sudden sense of urgency. It was not as if they could really do anything to help Maria—or *Mia*—now. It was in the hands of her government.

'I think they know what she can do,' said Donal, as they let themselves out into the stiff morning breeze a few minutes later. 'I think she *is* a phenomenon and they know it, so they do. They're going to use her for their own ends.'

Brigid squeezed his hand in hers, still instinctively careful, and then remembering that it was fine. Donal's hands were *fine*.

'Come on,' she said. 'Walk with me, old man.'

'Not so old today,' smiled Donal.

# 28

Dax Jones flew in swooping arcs, left and right of Mia's path. High above and silent. Mia did not look up. He knew Owen was right. He had not forgotten the moment when Mia's wall of flame had knocked them all off their feet. They had come running out of the wood because, as they talked beneath the tree house, Lisa had sensed something terrible.

He and Gideon had not known how seriously to take this because Lisa had been having a funny five minutes beforehand. She'd kept talking about someone spying on them. 'I can feel it!' she had said, as they'd walked across to the wood to find Mia. 'He's here!'

'Who's here?' Gideon had asked, staring around and up and down.

'I don't know . . . but . . . someone. No . . . gone,'

she sighed. 'I felt *certain* there was someone up in that tree!' She pointed to a high oak on the edge of a narrow spur of trees which struck out from the main area of their small wood. 'Certain! But not now. There's nobody now. OH!' She spun around and glared in the opposite direction, towards a row of cedars close to the complex where Chambers and the scientists worked. 'THERE!'

'Where?' asked Dax, ready to take flight and check it out.

'No—gone again,' sighed Lisa. 'Someone's messing with me. It's probably just some spirit I've upset,' she added, rubbing her left shoulder. It always got cold and achey when the spirits were agitating her.

'Well, that narrows the list down to several thousand,' observed Gideon.

But the feeling kept coming and she kept stopping, staring around, getting more and more aggravated. 'This is freaking me out!' she'd told them. 'I can't trust my own instincts any more!'

'Forget it,' Dax had said. 'It's more important to find Mia. She needs us. Ask Sylv to block whoever it is out.'

And they'd pushed on into the wood, only to

find Mia had gone. And then Lisa, looking stricken, had said, 'She doesn't want to see us. She's hiding from us.'

Dax scented something in the air which proved Lisa was right . . . but only partly right. Mia *wasn't* hiding from *them*. There was a bitter undertone of shame in her scent. She was hiding from their disgust. But she was wrong; they knew she could *never* willingly hurt someone; that it was a horrific accident. How could she think they would be disgusted with her?

They stood by the tree house for a while, talking. 'Maybe we should let her have some time alone,' Lisa said, forlornly. 'If she doesn't want to see us . . .'

'She's not alone,' Dax said suddenly, picking up the distinctive scent of the illusionist. 'She's with Spook. In the garden.'

'He's not good for her!' snarled Lisa. 'He's up to something! I've got to stop this.'

And then she started running—and Gideon and Dax, after glancing anxiously at each other, ran after her.

Into hell.

Mia and Spook were having some kind of scene by the rose arbour. Mia was hysterical and Spook was holding tightly onto her. Dax instinctively shifted to the falcon and rose up so he could see better. And then Mia had turned to them and he'd heard Spook yell, 'DO IT! DO IT NOW!' and then a wall of fire had blasted across the grass towards Lisa and Gideon.

They took the worst of it. They were sent flying backwards as if they'd been hit by a truck, both striking the unforgiving trunks of large trees as the inferno snarled after them. Dax spun high into the air on the blistering updraft. He landed on the far side of the Fenton Lodge roof and, filled with horror, struggled back into flight, rising up over the gable to see if this could truly be happening. Could Mia really have just tried to kill her best friends?

He didn't see much. As soon as he cleared the roof a column of white hot fire came directly for him, as if it had been aimed by a flame-thrower. If he hadn't been the fastest bird on the planet he would have been incinerated. As it was, when he landed again, deep in the wood, shaking and shocked almost senseless, his tail feathers were singed and smoking. He had shifted to a fox instinctively and gone to earth in an abandoned badger sett. He had dropped into the womb of soil and roots and passed out into oblivion.

In the evening he had emerged to watch the wreckage of Mia's attack being picked over by the military, under bright white arc lighting. The garden was a smoking wasteland and the wrought iron balustrades on the front steps of the lodge were melted. Even the windows were warped like boiled sugar.

The toll was terrible. Listening in from the roof, he learned that Spook was in lockdown, Lisa was hanging between life and death, and not just Gideon but *Luke* too . . . comatose. Luke had been close by when the fire attack happened, and had run through the flames to save his brother. Now their poor father was holding vigil for both sons. The healers had done all they could but none of them was as powerful as Mia. And Mia was gone.

Dax knew he should let them know he was alive. But he'd had a deeper need. Owen Hind. Pausing only to fly into his room and gather some emergency items from his bedside, he'd begun his long flight to Spain as soon as the dawn broke. And now . . . days later, here he was on the west coast of Ireland!

*Mia,* he sent, wishing with all his heart that she could hear him in her head, *I don't believe you meant to kill us! I don't believe it. Spook was doing something . . . making you see something. Tricking you.*

But Mia did not look up. She went on steadily climbing the mountain, occasionally pausing to stare thoughtfully into one hand as a small flame rose out of it like an orange dahlia blossom, and then snapping it away and moving on. *Is she the same person?* Dax wondered. Would she even recognize him?

Soon, he would find out. He couldn't bear the idea of a military search party reaching her first . . . or even Owen and Tyrone. He could never live with himself if they got hurt. No. He wanted the chance to talk to her. One on one. He owed her that.

Spook stayed up above the tideline, mindful of his Italian leather boots, while The Collector and Olu wandered along the water's edge. So this was where Mia had ended up. He felt a sour twist in his insides. Would he have gone through with the plan if he'd known it would work out like this? He hated to admit it, but he had underestimated the force of her power.

When Dax and Lisa and Gideon had come running out of the woods it had been easy to throw an illusion and disguise them as military men—he even cloaked Dax, as he shifted and flew up, as a distant helicopter. A moment of brilliance. It was a perfect way to convince Mia to escape with him—convincing her that the COLA Project military were turning on her. And he knew that if he made her start a fire in full view of these witnesses she would be persuaded there was no going back. 'I don't want her to feel she's been kidnapped,' The Collector had told him, weeks earlier. 'I want her to know she's been *rescued*.'

Spook had expected her to torch the grass and create a barrier to stop the three musketeers getting any closer. He had *not* expected her to blast a wall of flame directly at them—and then hurl a fire jet at Dax Jones. That had thrown him. But he'd recovered fast, telling himself they'd probably survive—COLAs were tough! And they'd have all the healers . . . except Mia, of course . . . sorting them out in no time.

And when Olu had at last shown up and grabbed Mia, he had expected to be grabbed too . . . and taken away with her to the safety and calm of The

Collector's hilltop home on the Faroe Islands. Only things had gone badly wrong. For a start, he had not yet sliced out his own magnetite lozenge. 'Her first,' he'd said, 'Then come back for me!' Olu nodded— but the second he'd laid his hands on Mia she must have set light to him. The boy's screams were still echoing in Spook's ears when they both vanished. He had stood amid the flames, alone and sick with shock. *She'll heal him, though,* he told himself. *As soon as she gets to The Collector and he explains what's happening. Then Olu will be back for me . . . any minute.* He went to find the scalpel, to cut out the magnetite, but then time seemed to speed up.

The *real* military men emerged, like ants from a kicked nest, and he knew he was only seconds away from lockdown on the Containment level. Olu would not be back in time. Cutting himself open now was pointless—and a problem if he was to play this new set of cards he'd been dealt. Spook quickly threw the blade deep into the flower bed, pasted on a look of shock, horror and innocence . . . and got ready for Containment.

And now, days later, he *had* been rescued . . . but the way the plan had fallen apart had dented his confidence enormously.

'She's still around here,' The Collector was saying, as he stepped up the beach with Olu at his side. 'I can sense her.' There was a strange light in his eyes. 'She's getting closer too. We need only wait. My Mia is nearly here.'

Olu and Spook exchanged looks. *My Mia?*

'Are you sure she won't set light to me again, Granite?' asked Olu.

The man patted his shoulder and replied, 'I'm not sure of anything. But I am very optimistic!'

'Why do you call him Granite?' asked Spook.

Olu shrugged. 'Why do *you* call him The Collector?'

'I go by both names,' said the man. 'But perhaps it's time to tell you my real name. I'm Marcus. Marcus Croft. You may call me whichever name you please.'

Again Spook and Olu looked at each other. Marcus Croft? It . . . seemed to suit him, thought Spook. And it was certainly easier to say than 'The Collector'.

'Marcus it is then,' he said.

'Marcus . . . ' said Olu, experimentally. 'Nah— I'll stick with Granite.'

'Let's walk,' said Marcus Croft, waving his hand

to the north end of the beach where the cliff rose high. 'I think it's this way.'

Tyrone met Owen at the crest of the foothill above the coast road, just in time to see Mia cross the thin ribbon of grey tarmac below and head towards the beach.

'We need to speed up!' puffed Owen, who had run uphill for the past ten minutes, while Tyrone had run down. 'Dax is flying above her still, but any time now he's going to drop down and shift—try to talk to her—I know it!'

'She seems calm,' Tyrone said, as they scrambled down the hillside, feet sliding on gravel and displaced clumps of peaty earth. 'No reason to think she'll hurt him.'

Owen said nothing, but climbed down faster. He hoped Tyrone was right.

'Stay here,' Chambers commanded Malone. 'I'm going after her now—and I *don't* want any backup, do you understand?'

'If you say so,' said Malone, looking bemused.

Chambers got out of the car, watching Mia's dark head bobbing along the top of some low vegetation at the far side of the road. She was making for the cliff path—perhaps to go down to the beach. This was good. The beach would be deserted at this time of the morning. As he crossed the road and began to follow he checked his inside jacket pocket and found two pens. One was his usual silver Scheaffer and the other was black and slightly thicker. Inside it was a syringe and a retractable needle. It could punch in a fast-acting sedative. It would drop Mia in three seconds.

He hoped he wouldn't need to use it, but even if she was calm and tractable with *him*—after all, she knew him well after nearly five years with Cola Club—she would most likely panic when the search patrol arrived, no matter how softly-softly the men trod. No . . . knocking her out was the safest option. It would give them time to get her back to Containment where she would remain sedated until her future was determined.

He ducked low amid the sprawling tussocks of seagrass, as she reached the edge of the cliff and looked left and right. He'd thought she would take the path down to the beach but instead she turned to her right and walked along the clifftop. He glanced up and saw a bird swoop in a curve high above and turn in the direction Mia was walking—to where the cliffs rose higher.

Chambers quickened his pace and then paused, as *she* paused to peer at the beach below. Then she sat down close to the edge, legs crossed and elbows on her knees. She seemed to be examining something in her hands. With a surge of shock he realized what it was. A *ball of fire*. So, the search patrol had been right. Jem had told him that he'd seen bright points of light from a distance. Mia was—quite literally—playing with fire.

He slowed his steps, thinking fast. Would she bowl the flames at him the moment he hailed her? He had to get closer. Walk right up to her and sit down at her side. Non-aggressive. No threat. He was . . . no threat at all. That was his angle.

Mia knew she was being followed. It didn't matter. Nobody was going to get close enough to stop her. There was a man along the cliff . . . someone she knew, but she wasn't sure who. There were more men—two of them—coming down the mountain slopes; nearly at the road. There were more people on the beach . . . three of them trekking along the water's edge and . . . two more some way behind them, ambling higher up along the shingle. What's more . . . someone was tracking her from above too. Or maybe that was just someone dowsing, because she could feel that telltale tickle in her scalp. Most likely Paulina Sartre because—obviously—Lisa was dead. A little dagger of pain got through the numbness then. She let the fire bloom out of her palm as a distraction.

The man along the clifftop was getting a bit too close. And the white-haired man down on the beach was now striding towards her, with two boys running to catch up with him. She sighed. She would have liked more time to think—to weigh up her life in case she discovered it *was* worth saving. But it was going to have to be now or never.

She stood up and stepped to the edge.

Dax saw what she meant to do and gave a screech before flipping over into a stoop and plummeting towards her. He hit the turf at the edge of the cliff and shifted into a boy, his arms flailing as he desperately tried to gain his balance. 'MIA!' he yelled. 'DON'T!'

Mia spun around and stared at him in utter amazement. She was holding a ball of fire in each palm and, as she moved, the flames suddenly shot upwards in two columns of flickering gold, red, and blue. Dax could feel the heat across his face.

'Dax . . . ?' she murmured, looking incredulous. 'You're not dead . . . '

'NO!' he yelled.

'But . . . I set fire to you all in the tree house!' she said, shaking her head. The columns of flame abruptly sucked back down into her palms, leaving nothing but a trail of smoke blown along the clifftop.

Dax was confused. The tree house had never caught alight.

'And I know Lisa is dead . . . or she would have dowsed me . . . ' went on Mia. 'I've killed people, Dax. Lots of people.'

'You haven't!' he yelled. 'Lisa is—'

But at that point Dax saw Chambers arrive at Mia's side. There was something in his hand—something pen-like. He was about to inject her with it. Dax's mouth fell open and he could not hide his dismay— even though he guessed Chambers was hoping he would play along and keep distracting Mia.

Mia, though, had no need of Dax's help. She smiled at him and flipped her hand backwards over her shoulder. At once the pen-like thing in Chambers' hand erupted into blue flame. He cursed and dropped it into the grass.

'Mia,' he began, his voice still remarkably low and calm. 'Please don't hurt yourself. Come home with Dax and me.'

'Home?' Mia stepped back a little so she could take both Dax and Chambers in. 'You want to take me *home*?' She gave a cold little laugh. 'Yes . . . I'm sure everyone at Fenton Lodge will welcome me with open arms after I killed Lisa and—'

'Lisa is fine,' said Chambers, waving his burnt fingers in the cold breeze and wincing only slightly. 'She's desperate to see you.'

Dax quailed at this. Lisa was not dead but she was very far from fine and he wished Chambers hadn't lied. Mia might not be psychic but she could still read people very well . . . sense infirmity and disease and emotional trauma. No matter how practised Chambers might be, she was narrowing her eyes at him now.

'You're lying,' she said.

And stepped off the cliff.

# 29

Owen and Tyrone reached the road and split up. 'One on either side—and close in carefully!' Owen said. He could see Mia at the edge of the cliff, Dax coasting the inshore breeze above her, and—to his dismay—someone making a beeline towards her from the south. Someone who looked remarkably like his old boss, David Chambers.

Tyrone struck out at an angle along the cliff, away from Mia, running fast but keeping low. He didn't plan to close in at all—he could read the body language even from here and he knew it would do no good. He could only help from distance. It was a long time since he'd attempted anything like this and he wasn't at all certain it would work. He found a small outcrop of rock and climbed a little way down it, before turning and settling his gaze on Mia as she stood at the edge of the cliff, arguing with Chambers and Dax—and turned, and . . .

Mia felt a cold sense of calm as she stepped off the cliff. There really was no other way. She dropped like a stone to shouts of horror from people on the cliff and down on the beach below . . . She had enough time to guess that she probably wasn't a goddess after all . . .

And then she stopped falling.

A metre above a large knuckle of rock which would surely have split her head in two, she simply stopped. It was as if she'd been caught in some kind of energy beam from a sci-fi show. She could still move her arms and legs but the falling had ended. She turned slowly back upright in the air, amazed. At first she wondered if she had done this herself . . . was it another power she had not realized she possessed? But then she sensed the pain and struggle of another human being and glanced along the cliff. Fifty metres away, a young man was sprawled on the edge, his hands outstretched, holding her there with his *mind*. With incredulity, she realized it was *Tyrone Lewis*, Gideon's old telekinetic tutor, who had stopped her fall.

Then he flopped down onto his face, exhausted, and she tumbled the last metre just in time to see Spook Williams tearing across the beach towards her, ahead of a white-haired man and a black teenage boy who looked vaguely familiar. Above, Dax and Chambers and—oh—now *Owen Hind*, peered down from the cliff. Some way behind them she could hear the shouts and calls of a military patrol cutting through the morning air.

And if she wasn't mistaken, wasn't that the old couple, unwisely hastening into the action, Brigid and Donal?

It was like a surprise party. *Mia Cooper! Meeting friends old and new!*

There was nothing else for it. Mia began to laugh. The sound was eerie and whooping and as she let it all out, a neat circle of fire, like something a witch would create in the woods, closed around her. All these players in her life . . . trying to convince her to do something. It was extraordinary how many people were determined to influence her.

'Mia! Mia! Oh thank God we've found you!' gasped Spook. 'Please—Mia. Let me help you. Before Chambers gets down here. Let me get you away from here!'

'What—with *him?*' Mia curled her lip at the boy behind Spook. Across her circle of fire she could see the evidence of their last encounter on the side of his face and one arm. 'You still want to give me a lift, do you?' she asked him. He looked afraid. And well he might.

Above her the COLA Project men were scrambling along the cliff path, desperate to get down to her. She was untroubled. There was time enough for anything when you could bend your own element. The sense of power and control was exhilarating. For years she had felt at the mercy of her healing power . . . made weak and vulnerable by it; for ever trying to cloak the Effect; embarrassed, awkward. But now . . .

'Come on then, Spook,' she invited, making a small gateway in the flames. 'Come in and see me.'

Spook hesitated, glancing at the fiery perimeter uneasily, but the white-haired man behind him tapped his shoulder and said, 'Go in, Spook.'

He looked good, she thought, distantly. Tall and rangy in his usual black jeans and expensive boots, his cheeks a little hollow and his amber eyes shining and intense. As soon as he stepped through the little gateway she closed it and sent

231

the flames several metres high, enclosing them both in an untouchable bubble. He jerked around, staring fearfully up at the shimmering white and gold haze.

'Are you . . . are you going to cook us both?' he said, attempting to be light. She could see the terror behind his eyes though.

'No,' she said. 'The heat won't touch you. Sit down. Talk to me.'

He regained some of his swagger then, and settled down next to her. 'Mia . . . I've been frantic about you. Are you OK?' He reached a hand towards her face but something in her look froze the hand midway.

'Don't I look OK?' she asked, smiling.

He gulped. 'You look amazing. Beautiful. Look what you've become!'

'Yes,' said Mia. 'Look what I've become. And you, Spook, you helped, didn't you?'

He shrugged and smiled down at the sand, wiping a little of it off his Italian leather boots. 'I just . . . encouraged you to be your true self.'

'Yes—you helped me become a killer,' she said.

'No!' He looked stung, hurt. 'You didn't kill anyone . . . well, not deliberately. That was a mistake . . . and self-defence. You don't have to worry about that.'

'You used illusion, didn't you?' she said. 'To make me see things that weren't there. To make me attack people.'

'No—no, of course not!' he blustered. She could *smell* the sweat on him.

'I'm sure you thought it was for the best,' she went on.

'It was! It *is*! We're here to rescue you now—and soon you'll see! Everything's going to be fine. We'll be together. We'll . . . '

'Kiss me,' she said, calling a sudden halt to his babbling. 'Like you did before. Remember?'

He took a breath—a shaky one—and carefully put his hands on her shoulders, pulling her towards him.

'Wait though,' she said, her face close to his. 'I should warn you . . . it might be hot.'

Again, the fear flickered through him. He kissed her anyway. And she set fire to his boots.

A tiny gap opened in the wall of flame and Spook ran out, screaming. To say he was in a hurry was an understatement. Dax, flying above, saw his old foe hurtle down the beach, his feet ablaze, and throw himself into the sea. The white-haired man he'd come with watched with interest and then turned back to the fire chamber and stepped through the gap.

Marcus sat down. 'Hello, Mia,' he said, directing cool blue eyes at her. 'I've been wanting to meet you for the longest time.'

'You ought to be careful,' she warned, bringing the ring of flames down to just a couple of metres. 'I could flash-fry you.'

'Yes, you could,' he said. 'But you won't. After all, that's no way to treat family.'

She narrowed her eyes at him. It was a good line, she had to admit.

'Take my hand and you'll know,' he said. 'You can read physical make-up, yes? Then read mine. I don't need you to find any aches and pains . . . just check out the DNA.' He held out one hand, palm up.

*Why not?* She took his hand.

The jolt of recognition made her suck in a lungful of salty air.

'Hello, Mia,' he said, smiling.

'Hello, Granddad,' she replied.

# 30

Outside the circle of fire the world was getting closer. Chambers and his men were now yomping along the beach, having found a path down. Owen Hind was running alongside them. Chambers spared him an astonished glance and then shook his head. This day could not get any stranger. But if he did not focus he would lose Mia to Marcus Croft.

They reached the fire circle and saw, through chinks in the flames, that Croft was inside it with her. Chambers wished the man would go up in smoke but as Mia was holding his hand and staring into his eyes it looked like he wasn't toast just yet.

'You might be able to take Croft down,' said Chambers to Jem, who immediately ordered his men to take aim. 'Injured, preferably.' But if nothing else got any better today, Chambers would be happy to at least chalk up the death of Croft.

'How did you let this happen?' Owen was shaking his head beside Chambers. 'You've lost the plot.'

Chambers stared at him. 'This coming from a dead man,' he said, coldly. He had liked Hind and respected him a great deal. His grief at the man's funeral had been genuine—and it hit him hard to realize he'd been duped. 'And what would the undead suggest?' he added, acidly.

'Let Dax talk to her,' said Owen. The boy was back in falcon form, turning in the air above.

'She tried to blast him out of the sky before, didn't he mention?' said Chambers.

'I think we both know she was misdirected by Spook. And don't you think it's time you got *him* back?' Owen nodded across to the boy, standing in the shallows, examining his ruined boots and yelping with pain.

'See how close he is to Olu Jackson?' asked Chambers. Olu was at the water's edge, anxiously glancing between Spook and what could be seen of Marcus Croft amid Mia's flames. 'If we take a step towards him, Olu will teleport Spook to another country. And if we try to storm Mia and get her away from Croft, she'll probably torch us all. You see my difficulty? Now . . . our good friend Tyrone, on the other hand, might be able to help.'

Owen saw Tyrone making his way down the cliff path at the far end of the beach and his heart quailed. Some kind of *Clash of the Titans* scene would be unfolding soon if Chambers had his way. He could lose everyone he cared about on this beach.

He gave a mirthless chuckle. 'However we look at it, David, the terrible fact is . . . that day has come. You're no longer in control.'


'You're my mother's father?' Mia said, staring at a face which was becoming more familiar to her with every blink.

'Yes,' said the man. 'My name is Marcus Croft. I'm sorry it's taken me so long to find you. If I had known about you sooner—'

'Doesn't matter now,' said Mia. 'What do you want?'

'I want my granddaughter,' he said. 'And you . . . you need someone to help you be . . . amazing.'

'You think I need help?' she asked.

'Do you think there's still help for you at Cola Club?'

Mia smiled, sadly. 'I may be new to fire-starting,' she said. 'But I haven't cooked my own brain.'

Just outside the fire, Dax landed and shifted to the fox. His hearing sharpened dramatically and beyond the soft hiss of the flames he picked up the conversation inside.

Mia knew he was there. And that was fine. It might help them all understand.

'So—come with me. You'll be in good company, with Spook and Olu. Even though,' her grandfather smiled and raised an eyebrow, 'I gather, you're a little cross with them both right now. You'll forgive them in time. And more COLAs will come to us— of their own free will. Maybe even your friends. With me, you need never fear being locked down and drugged. I am not afraid of you. I am *thrilled* by what you can do. Come with me.'

'What makes you think I need to go anywhere with anyone?' she replied. 'Wouldn't you say I can look after myself?' She mirrored that raised eyebrow.

'You don't want to live that kind of life,' he said, his voice soft and full of knowledge. 'Outcast, alone, set apart. You still need love, Mia. Family love. The kind that lasts through thick and thin.

And I think we both know you can't get that at Cola Club any more.'

'I could have had it,' she said, looking at him coldly. 'If you and Spook hadn't decided to change my future.'

'Mia, my love,' he replied. 'It was only ever a matter of time before your true nature revealed itself. And keeping it all in . . . well that wasn't doing you any good, was it?'

Mia said nothing. She knew this was true. She stared around at her igloo of flame and wondered exactly *how* she was going to make her exit. At least, once she had gone, there would be no more deaths. And she wanted to find out more from this man. *Her grandfather.* He could tell her everything he knew about her mother . . . Already she felt that sense of weightlessness, of dissolving, which had begun with her father's death, begin to lessen. She should go now, with her grandfather, before anyone else got hurt. But first she had to know whether Lisa was dead or alive. And Gideon, too . . . Perhaps she could get Dax in here to talk to her next. It was getting tenser by the minute out there, with all the soldiers, but Chambers would probably allow Dax in.

'MARIA!' yelled a familiar voice.

Brigid and Donal had seen the fire but it wasn't until they got closer and saw the British military that they realized Mia was inside it. They began to run. As well as the military there seemed to be random strangers all over the beach. Mia was in danger. Why was nobody helping her? Why were these men poised all around her with rifles at aim?

Mia, inside the flaming circle, eye to eye with a brand new grandfather, heard the familiar Irish accent of the man who had found her on the tideline.

'Maria!' he called. 'What have they done to you, chick?'

Mia stood up, pushing the flames down to ankle height, and yelled, 'DONAL! NO—STAY BACK! STAY BACK!'

But the man still came running—and she heard guns being readied by Chambers' patrol, despite shouts from both Chambers and Owen.

There was a shot and Donal dropped onto the sand.

Mia's world went very quiet—even though the

dry seaweed for a mile along the tideline suddenly burst into dark smoking flames and every wielded weapon melted, amid cries of pain from the patrol.

Mia walked towards him and even Brigid stopped coming. She stood frozen, her hands to her mouth. Mia was dimly aware of an intense brightness and everyone backing away from her, eyes wide with shock. *I'm like a Roman candle!* she thought. *I'm blazing!* The fire was rippling out of her hands, arms, and shoulders and twisting high into the air. She knelt down next to Donal, who was shot in the chest. He was sucking in air and staring at her in astonishment as the blood welled up through his old coat. She pressed her palm to the wound. The top of her hand blazed on, but the palm was only warm. She felt the echo of the bullet in her own chest and then felt the actual bullet thud against her palm as it pulled clear of his flesh. Then she closed her eyes and sent in the healing.

When it was done she turned to face the astonished, scared crowd around her. The fire fanned out of her head, shoulders, back . . . rising up in hot wings of rainbow colours. 'I'm done with all of this,' she said, looking towards Chambers. 'I have plans and I don't need your help. Except you,' she pointed to Dax. 'And you,' she pointed to Olu. 'Get rid of them first,' she said, waving at the white-haired man and Spook, who was barefoot, blistered, still swaying with pain at the water's edge. 'And come back.'

Olu stared at Granite. 'Do it,' said Granite. And Olu took Spook and Granite away.

He was back in five seconds. 'Now what, sister?' he said, trying to sound unafraid.

'Dax,' said Mia. 'Come here.'

Dax shifted to boy shape. 'Say goodbye to Owen,' she said.

Dax gulped. He had no idea what was about to happen. Owen made to move towards him but Chambers held him back.

'Take us both,' said Mia, to Olu. 'To the medical unit at Fenton Lodge.'

'We might never get out again,' warned Olu.

'Oh, we will,' said Mia, taking his hand. 'We will.'

# 31

'Please don't move, Janey,' said Dax, the second his head had cleared. 'It'll be OK.'

The doctor looked frozen anyway. But she murmured, 'Mia! Oh, Mia!'

Mia sat down next to Lisa and took her hand. She was no longer ablaze, but there was an unearthly glow around her. She closed her eyes and Dax and Olu watched as the blisters and scars along Lisa's face slowly paled and smoothed until the girl's skin was unmarked. Mia noted that the pain of healing seemed less intense now. In the past, healing her friends or her father had always been the most painful and difficult experience. Not any more. It seemed her grandfather was right. Now that her dark side was no longer hidden she seemed to be whole. 'Wake up,' said Mia and Lisa's eyes opened.

They immediately filled with tears and she tried to reach up for her best friend.

But Mia stood and moved away to the room at the far end where Gideon and Luke lay. Dax followed her. Janey wandered across to Lisa and unwound the bandages on her arms. Beneath them lay perfectly healed skin. By the time the doctor reached Luke and Gideon's room, they too were healed and open-eyed. Michael Reader sat in his chair between their two beds, speechless and dazed, and Dax was patting his best friend's shoulder, grinning at him.

Mia looked at the twin brothers and said, 'I'm sorry. I didn't mean to.'

Then she turned to Dax. 'Did I hurt anyone else? There was a helicopter, I think.'

He shook his head. 'No—no helicopter. I think that might have been me—in one of Spook's disguises. You were misdirected, Mia. It was never your fault.'

Mia returned to Lisa. On the way she paused by Olu, almost casually trailing her hand along his face and shoulder. His skin healed in the wake of her fingers. Then she was back at Lisa's side. Dax watched the best friends stare at each other. He felt his heart sink. He could not see a happy ending for Mia, no matter how many people she made better.

'I *knew* you'd come back,' said Lisa. 'I *knew* it! From the minute that man tried to get in my head and find you!'

Mia smiled sadly. 'I'm not back,' she said. 'I can't stay.'

'Of *course* you're back!' Lisa sat up with a jerk, in spite of Janey's concerned noises. 'You belong with us, here at Cola Club! We'll make everything all right! It'll be just like it used to be!'

Mia looked at Dax. 'Tell her,' she said.

'She can't stay,' he said, his voice thick with sadness. His throat seemed to be closing in on itself. He could not believe this was truly happening.

'Dax! Don't be stupid!' Lisa looked furious and terrified. 'What's got into you? Mia belongs with us!'

There was a noise at the door.

'Janey, stop them!' said Mia. 'Just for a minute.'

Janey leaned against the door. 'Hold on, boys,' she called. 'We're fine in here. Don't come in until I give you the all-clear.'

Dax nodded at Olu. 'Get her out of here,' he said, unable to keep the shake out of his voice. Olu stepped across.

'I'll never forget you,' said Mia, taking Lisa's hand and reaching for Dax's. 'And I hope I'll see you again one day. But I think I belong with my grandfather now—and if not . . . well, I'll find somewhere else. I won't risk killing anyone I care about by staying here. And I won't be caged and drugged, either.'

'Mia . . . please . . . ' sobbed Lisa. 'You're my best friend . . . I can't do without you!'

'You'll do fine,' said Mia, disengaging her hands from Lisa and Dax. Her voice was hard but Dax saw that her eyes were wet, just before Olu grabbed her shoulder and there was nothing left.

A second later the door was smashed in.

# 32

'We could use you,' said Chambers. 'More than ever now.'

Owen and Tyrone exchanged glances as Chambers' helicopter appeared on the horizon.

'I don't think we're cut out to serve Her Majesty these days,' said Owen.

'I could have you both arrested and detained indefinitely,' pointed out Chambers, indicating the patrol debriefing along the beach.

'It would be fun to see you try,' said Tyrone.

'Dear God, let's not start locking horns already,' said Owen. 'You have a crisis but the worst is past for the moment. Janey says Dax is safe—and now Lisa, Gideon, and Luke are healed. Mia did the only thing she could do, you know that, David.'

Chambers nodded, staring out to where the

tideline still smouldered. 'Don't think that a part of me isn't glad, Owen. I'm not a machine. But Mia . . . out there with that power, with *Marcus Croft*! With Olu and Spook Williams too . . . It's terrifying. What will they make her do?'

Owen remembered Mia, awash with golden flame like a fiery angel, healing the old man with the gunshot wound. 'I think you're looking at it the wrong way,' he said. 'Imagine what Mia might make *them* do.'

# 33

Lisa, Dax, and Gideon lay in the grass, staring into the sky and soaking up the last of the summer's sun.

'It suits you,' said Gideon. 'It's . . . kind of sixties hippy chick, like that model—Sticky.'

'Twiggy, you idiot!' said Lisa. She ran a hand through her short golden crop. 'But thanks anyway.'

High above them a vapour trail cut across the blue sky; some jet on its way around the world.

'Where do you think she is now?' murmured Dax.

'Could be anywhere,' said Gideon. 'Anywhere in the world. She's free.'

Lisa snorted. 'She's shackled to Spook Williams! How is that free?'

'No,' said Dax, sitting up. 'You didn't see her on the beach at the end. Lisa . . . you have to know . . .

she was . . . strong. Amazing. Calling all the shots. No more frail Mia. I've never seen her like that. She was like . . . a goddess.'

Lisa got up on one elbow and stared at him. 'So . . . you don't think Spook will suck her over to the . . . dark side?'

'I don't think Spook was ever capable of that,' said Dax. 'The fire thing started well before he got close to her. And we all knew—if we're going to be honest about it—that it would come back one day. It's part of her. If she didn't use it she was out of balance. I think that's why she struggled so hard with healing sometimes. She suffered . . . because she was repressing the fire thing.'

'Oh hark at Dr Dax Freud,' muttered Gideon.

'I miss her,' said Lisa. 'Life will never be the same again.'

'We're COLAs,' said Dax, putting his arm around her and kissing the top of her fluffy head. 'It never is.'

Ali Sparkes was a journalist and BBC broadcaster until she chucked in the safe job to go dangerously freelance and try her hand at writing comedy scripts. Her first venture was as a comedy columnist on *Woman's Hour* and later on *Home Truths*. Not long after, she discovered her real love was writing children's fiction.

Ali grew up adoring adventure stories about kids who mess about in the woods and still likes to mess about in the woods herself whenever possible. She lives with her husband and two sons in Southampton, England. Check out www.alisparkes.com for the latest news on Ali's forthcoming books.

## ACKNOWLEDGEMENTS:

With grateful thanks to Liz Cross and Claire Westwood for their clever guidance on this and the whole Unleashed story.

And to the lovely people of Ireland's west coast for inspiring the setting of *The Burning Beach*. And to Laura Trant for taking me to the seaweed baths ...

And finally, thank you Sarah Parish and James Scott Murray, for supplying the lovely Nell.